KING
OF
Lincoln Park

Book 7 of the Kings of the Castle Series

Book 1 is the Introduction

Books 2-9 are standalones

Martha Kennerson

Kennerson Books
League City, Texas

King of Lincoln Park by Martha Kennerson Copyright ©2019

Macro Publishing Group ISBN: (Ebook) 978-1-7331782-9-7
Kennerson Books ISBN: (Trade Paperback) 978-0-9894546-6-7

www.marthakennerson.com

Cover Designed by: J.L Woodson: www.woodsoncreativestudio.com
Interior Designed by: Lissa Woodson: www.naleighnakai.com
Editor: Lissa Woodson: www.naleighnakai.com

Manufactured and Printed in the United States of America

KING

OF

Lincoln Park

Book 7 of the Kings of the Castle Series

Book 1 is the Introduction

Books 2-9 are standalones

Martha Kennerson

♦ DEDICATION ♦

This book is dedicated to all the readers who have and continue to support my writing. You're all wonderful and I really appreciate your steadfast support.

♦ ACKNOWLEDGEMENTS ♦

I'd like to thank my own personal king, the love of my life, my best friend and husband who happily shares me with all these crazy characters that live in my head. Love you, honey.

Many thanks to my Tribe for being there with me. Anita L. Roseboro and Ellen Kiley Goeckler, thank you for pulling through for me on that last part getting this to print. Thank you to my "shared son" J. L. Woodson, for the awesome book cover. To my friend, editor, and agent, Naleighna Kai (Lissa Woodson), thank you for taking this journey with me.

CHAPTER 1

"Can you believe his pompous ass?" Grant asked his friend and business associate as they entered the hotel suite. Grant Khambrel, architect and owner of one of the country's premier construction companies, with a reputation for being an honorable and fair businessman, just had that reputation threatened by a man who had no qualms about using his position to get what he wanted.

"Yes, I can. We're dealing with a corrupt alderman for the largest ward in Chicago who's used to getting his way no matter the means," Montgomery stated, his annoyance clear.

Alderman James Knight, one of fifty aldermen serving four-year terms, also held positions as city councilman, real estate tycoon, and self-proclaimed Godfather of Chicago. While the man was handsome, in his mid-fifties, and in great shape, he was also arrogant enough to think he could bend everyone to his will.

Grant and his construction company was awarded a five-hundred-million-dollar contract to renovate and expand the United Center—home of the Chicago Bulls and Blackhawks. Allegations state that Grant failed to disclose a previous relationship with the principals of the project, which automatically disqualified him for the award. Even though the assertion was not true, the alderman was blackmailing

Grant. He wanted something that Grant has which will require him to betray his mentor, Khalil Germaine.

He moved across the eloquently designed room toward the mirrored bar situated in the corner. The cream walls with mirrored accents, red curtains, and dainty furnishings were a bit too feminine for his taste. The room was fit more for a queen than a king, and the irony in that fact was not lost on Grant. Although he did appreciate the hospitality of the Hotel Chicago as he eyed the bottle of Louis XIII Cognac, they'd gifted him.

"Want a drink?" Grant removed the jacket to his gray Armani suit and tossed it across the arm of the white sofa.

Meeks checked his watch, and it was barely ten in the morning. "Sure, it's five o'clock somewhere." He took off his Giovanni suit jacket, draped it over one of the matching wingback chairs facing the sofa. "How's Uncle Ben?"

Grant felt a dull but consistent pain in his chest. His uncle, Benjamin Khambrel, Ben, as he preferred being called, raised Grant after his parents died in a car crash. Despite the liquid burning down his throat, his mind flew back to the time when his life had changed forever. He was ten years old when a drunk driver killed his parents. Grant stood in front of two identical caskets wearing a black suit holding the hand of a man who was the mirror image of his father, but who Grant had mostly seen on holidays. Thanksgiving was Grant's favorite time—his parents played with him while his uncle did all the cooking.

Crying and wondering why his life had to change, he whispered, "This isn't fair."

Uncle Ben looked down at his heartbroken nephew, wiped away the tears, and said, "No, it's not. It's just you and me now, kid. I'll take good care of you."

Up until then, Grant had lived in a big house in his hometown of Houston, Texas. He had two parents who loved him and whom he loved, with lots of friends who understood him. Now the world as he knew it was over. From that day forward, Grant's uncle kept his word and had taken good care of him. As a single gay man, Ben had to make a lot of adjustments and sacrifices to fit a scared and impressionable ten-year-old boy into his life. Grant loved him dearly for it.

His uncle had raised him in Lincoln Park, a neighborhood in Chicago. They lived in a condo nestled in a tree-lined community surrounded by diverse nightlife, art galleries, along with upscale and culturally rich restaurants. The northern area was the perfect setting for his uncle, who was a chef with a big personality. While Ben was discreet about his lifestyle, for a shy, gifted boy, who had just lost his parents, making sense of the new environment had been difficult.

"You okay, Grant?" Meeks asked.

Bringing his attention back to the conversation, he replied, "Uncle Ben is still fighting an aggressive form of cancer. We're waiting for the results from his last set of scans, but we have every reason to think positive."

"That's great news, man. And Khalil?"

Khalil Germaine, the founder of Macro International Magnet School, was Grant's former mentor and teacher. Not only had he taught philosophy and science, he'd taught subjects outside of the normal curriculum. Life skills that busy or sometimes absent parents tended to forget to impart in their children, such as balancing a checkbook, preparing for adulthood, managing crises, among other basic things like maintaining a residence and advocating for what they needed on a personal level.

Another unpleasant memory took flight, forcing him to relive the moment.

Grant received a late-night call regarding his mentor from a number he didn't recognized.

"Grant Khambrel."

"Mr. Khambrel, this is Katrina White, and I'm a nurse at Northwestern Memorial Hospital in Wilmette."

"How can I help you?"

"I'm actually calling to advise you that there's been an incident, and Khalil Germaine has been admitted."

Grant's heart rate increased at the thought of someone he hadn't been in touch with for years being injured.

"What kind of incident?"

"Mr. Germaine is in critical condition. You're listed as one of his emergency contacts. Can you come?" Grant's knees buckled, and he perched on the edge of his desk. Khalil was as much of a second father to him as his uncle had been.

Grant fought back his fear and found his words. "Yes, of course." He stood and grabbed a note pad from his desk. "I'll get there as soon as I can." After jotting down all the pertinent information, he disconnected the call, rounded his desk, and placed his things in his briefcase with one hand while he dialed his pilot with the other.

"Excuse me, Nurse…" Grant read the name tag of the nurse at the patient information center when he arrived. "Mary. Isn't there anything you can tell me about Khalil Germaine's condition? He's my father."

"Your father," she repeated, her left eyebrow raised, skepticism front and center.

"Yes, I'm Mr. Germaine's son, and I need to know his condition." Grant's voice raised an octave, and then he heaved a sigh. "My

apologies, I'm just worried about my father."

"I understand. Let me see what I can find out." She stood, maneuvered around the desk. "Excuse me for a moment."

Grant turned and leaned against the nurses' station.

"Mr. Khambrel..."

"Yes."

"This way, please."

"Of course, but what can you tell me about my father's condition?" He followed her down the hall, where signs indicated they were headed toward the ICU. They stopped in front of a set of double doors. "Please..."

"All I can tell you is when Mr. Germaine arrived, he was in critical condition. They got him stabilized, and now he's in surgery." She swiped her badge across a scanner, and the silver doors flew open. "Follow me."

Grant felt as if he'd been hit in the chest. He flexed his whole body to stay upright.

"Mr. Khambrel, are you coming?" He looked up to see Nurse Mary on the other side of the door, standing and waiting for him.

"Yes." Grant quickly made it to her side, and she led him to a warmly decorated waiting room down from the ICU.

"You can wait here. The doctor will come find you when it's time."

"Thank you," he said as he watched Nurse Mary leave the room. Grant stood fighting his fears in the middle of the empty space, berating himself for not answering Khalil's call to action much sooner. It might have prevented the assassination attempt.

Grant was happy to share this update. "Khalil's much better, and he'll be going home soon." He handed Meeks a crystal goblet with a gold liquid and two cubes of ice.

"Thanks. Khalil will need security," Meeks said over the rim of his glass. "You don't want a repeat of what happened."

"No, we don't. Daron already has it under control," Grant assured before checking an incoming text message.

For years, Daron Kincaid, under the street moniker The Warden, was the brains behind an illegal organization with the sole purpose of taking down an international crime ring from the inside. With his "cloak and dagger" lifestyle behind him, Daron, a successful businessman who designed personal security gadgets for women, ensured the safety of The Castle and its Kings. Part of that safety included the new tattoo on Grant's inner wrist, a tracking device that he could activate in an emergency.

"I'm here if you need back-up." Meeks took another sip of his drink. "Now as for as Alderman Knight is concerned, you have to keep your cool."

"I am cool," Grant declared, sounding like a character from his uncle's favorite movie *Be Cool*. He tossed back his drink, barely letting his tongue experience the strong, smooth substance, as he moved back over to the bar. "Where does he get off thinking he can blackmail me, and I'll just roll over and let it happen?"

"You mean he thinks *we'll* just let it happen. He's messing with *our* money, too," Meeks admitted. "The Blake sisters don't play when it comes to family and their company, trust me. We consider you family, too."

Grant did trust his friends. Meeks Montgomery and his wife, Francine Blake Montgomery, were partners in their family's multibillion-dollar international security firm. The two men had met and bonded over a business deal several years earlier. Now another deal could dismantle everything if a dishonest alderman didn't get what he wanted.

"So how do you suggest we handle the good old alderman?" Grant poured himself another drink, thinking of a few things he'd love to try. He held up the bottle. "Refill?"

Meeks raised his glass. "I'm good." Meaning, one of them had to keep his head on straight.

"So, what do we do about Alderman Knight?" He asked before sitting on the sofa. "Besides laying hands on him, that is."

Meeks shook his head before taking a seat on one of the matching wingback chairs. "I swear, you're sounding more and more like Robert these days."

Robert Gold was Meeks' business partner and brother-in-law, who had little patience for nonsense. He believed with the proper physical motivation; people would do the right thing. Who would've thought the man was a computer genius and a proud geek?

"Yeah, well, where's Robert when I need him?" Grant reclined in his seat and took a sip of his drink. He glanced out of the balcony window and marveled at the City's skyline. It reminded him of the downtown view from his office in Texas.

"Robert's on another gig right now, and his method of handling things isn't what we need."

"No? Then what do you suggest? There's no way in hell I'm going to help him take the Castle away from Khalil. Hell, I couldn't even if I tried."

Meeks forehead creased. "The alderman didn't say he wanted to take the Castle, he wants access to it," he clarified.

Grant could almost see the thoughts swirling around in Meeks' head. He was clearly pondering something, but what? "What are you thinking?"

"Why *does* he want access to the Castle so bad? And, if he's not the one blackmailing you about your past, then who is?"

"That's the million-dollar question, don't you think? Or should I say five hundred million dollars since that's the amount we could lose if I don't give in to this bastard's demands." Grant reached for his ringing cell phone.

"Grant Khambrel."

"Mr. Khambrel, this is April Lowe, Autumn Knight's administrative assistant."

Grant sat up, his body coming alert at the mere mention of the name of the beautiful woman he'd yet to meet. "Miss Lowe, what can I do for you?" He could feel Meeks' eyes bore into his face.

"I was wondering what time you'd like to convene with Miss Knight in the morning. As the winning architect, we assumed you would want to take another tour before the winning construction company comes to impose their will," she said, and a touch of sarcasm tainted her tone.

Imposing their will. She doesn't know I'm the contractor, too. "I'm sure I can handle things."

"We hope so, sir. The contractor will be here at ten, so will eight-thirty work?"

"That will be fine, Miss Lowe, thank you."

"Thank you, and we'll see you in the morning Mr. Khambrel."

"What's up?" Meeks placed his empty glass on the coffee table next to a unique looking plant that captured his attention.

Grant placed his phone on his hip. "That was Miss Knight's office, she's the administrative director at the United Center, they wanted to confirm my arrival tomorrow."

"Miss Knight?" Meeks frowned. "Any relation to Alderman

Knight?"

Grant nodded. "Remember that gorgeous photo he showed off of his daughter at the first meeting?"

"Yeah."

Grant's heart skipped a beat, and his pants suddenly felt tight at the groin, just thinking about her beautiful smile. The photo the man had flashed didn't do her justice. "Well, she's also the woman from the hospital I told you about."

"The stranger you never got to meet, right?" Meeks stood and reached for his jacket.

"The very same." He stared up at his friend with a confused look. "Where the hell are you going?"

He picked up Grant's jacket and tossed it over. "We're going to go find a steak and formulate our plans."

"We just ate." Grant stood and put on his jacket.

"That was a snack." He placed his index finger over his lips and picked up the small plant that sat on the table. He raised it to the ceiling, turned it towards Meeks, showing him the electronic listening device attached. "Besides, I'm a growing boy."

Grant's expression hardened as he fought to keep his anger under control. "Boy, my ass. Where to?"

"We'll figure it out. Let's go," Meeks said, moving toward the door.

CHAPTER 2

"What the hell's going on?" Grant asked, trying to keep his anger under control and his voice down as they wound their way through the hotel lobby. The idea that someone had bugged his room was insane. Not even the attention of several beautiful women they passed could grab his attention.

"That's a good question." Meeks pulled out his phone. "We sure as hell are going to find out."

The two men walked into the hotel's lounge and took a seat facing the door, but away from any other patrons. "Why would someone feel the need to listen in on my conversations? It's not like I work out of the hotel. Hell, how did anyone even know where I'd be staying?"

"More good questions that need answering." Meeks' voice had a hard edge to it, as well it should.

"Hello, gentlemen, welcome to Hotel Chicago. My name is Sally," a pretty brunette greeted, eyeing both men but paying extra attention to Grant. Meeks' platinum wedding ring was hard to miss. "May I get you anything?"

"Two coffees, black, and some privacy, please," Grant stated in a matter-of-fact tone sending the message that now wasn't the time. He'd make sure she received a good tip to make up for his abruptness but right now Grant was ready to explode.

"Did Marie make your travel arrangements?"

"Yes, just like always. Except…" Grant frowned.

"Except what?" Meeks prompted.

Sally delivered their coffee and complimentary sweet buns, quickly taking her leave after advising the men to call out if they needed anything.

"What?" Meeks prompted.

"Marie coordinated the hotel arrangements with Miss Knight's office. The hotel was recommended for its quality and proximity to the facility which was only three miles away," Grant explained, reaching for his cup.

"Miss Knight, as in Alderman's Knight daughter." Meeks grimaced. "Your mystery woman. Damn, it looks like that beautiful apple might not have fallen far from a rotten tree."

Grant felt a pain in his chest that he'd never experienced before. He fought back, not wanting to deal with the implication. The father might be immoral, but it didn't mean she has to be.

Meeks' cell rang. "Jed, I need you to run a background check and do a security sweep for me."

Grant sat back, drinking his coffee and eating a sweet bun while Meeks held a conversation with Jed Shield who'd been a specialist with the firm for years. He still couldn't believe how crazy the last several days had been. First, his business and reputation are threatened by blackmail. Then his mentor was shot sending him running from Texas to Chicago. To top things off, his hotel room has been bugged by an unknown source that could be related to the one woman who's made him feel things he hadn't in a very long time—want and need.

"That's taken care of." Meeks said, placing his phone face down on the table then reaching for his coffee.

"What did you do?"

"My Chicago team's running a deep background check on the good alderman and going over to your hotel suite to do a sweep."

"Good, the more we know about Alderman Knight, the better."

"And his daughter," Meeks added, studying his friend.

Grant's jaw tightened, and he gave a quick nod. He hated thinking something unsavory would be discovered about the woman he'd yet to meet, but had played a starring role in his dreams.

"You actually think they planted more?" Grant shook his head and frowned before he silenced his ringing phone after checking the screen.

"What's wrong now?"

"Nothing, it's Jill."

Meeks smirked. "She's still hanging on, I see."

Jill Fox was a beautiful corporate attorney with whom Grant had a brief affair. He shrugged. "She's coming to town and wants to get together."

"She's coming to Chicago? Damn, talk about special delivery service." Meeks laughed.

"No, she's coming to Texas."

"Why the look?"

Grant rubbed his hands together. "There's no look, I'm not interested. Besides, I have enough going on, and I don't need the distraction."

"Oh, I think you do," Meek's teased. "I think you want one pretty bad. Only Jill doesn't fit the bill."

His friend was right, Jill wasn't the one he wanted, but Grant also wasn't ready to deal with that fact either, so he pivoted. "What do you think Jed's going to find?"

Meeks got the message, raised his hand, and gestured for the waitress. "You never know."

"Since when did you get a Chicago team?"

Sally eagerly returned, asking, "Have you gentlemen decided what you want?" She offered Grant a suggestive smile that indicated that she knew exactly what she wanted. Meeks was right. Grant usually wouldn't mind indulging in a no-strings-attached affair to take the edge off, especially when he was feeling stressed. Autumn Knight's beautiful face popped in his head, and Sally's offer died on the vine, as his uncle would to say. A colloquialism his uncle used against him whenever he'd come to him with an idea that he thought might be crazy or dangerous. He'd been very protective of his nephew.

"I'll have the steak, medium rare with a baked potato all the way."

"Make that two," Grant amended.

"No problem," she said, walking away, swinging her hips in a seductive manner.

"So, you have a Chicago office?" Grant repeated, reaching for his napkin. "And why didn't I know about it?"

"It seems there's a lot about each other's business we don't know," Meeks reminded him.

Grant frowned. "Man chill, it's not like you were hurting for business."

"Whatever. Business picked up in this area, so Francine and Farrah decided a local presence was needed." Meeks took a bite of his sweet bun. "Now tell me about this Castle and why the alderman wants it so damn bad."

"Money and influence," Grant explained. "On all points of the spectrum, runs through the Castle like water in the Chicago River. The Castle had been a place where wealthy people indulged in any and everything their hearts desired. Only a small percentage of that had a sexual slant, but Khalil found out that several illegal activities were flowing through the Castle. That was something he never intended and was determined to end." Grant winced, thinking about what his mentor had endured the moment he touched down on American soil. Two bullets meant to end his life.

"There has to be a reason why the alderman would go so low."

"You're right, and I have no idea why, but I'm sure as hell going to find out," Grant said as he watched Sally approach with their food.

While the two men enjoyed their meal, they discussed the hornets' nest of criminal activities they suddenly found themselves affiliated with, and different ways to dissociate from all parties involved. Grant watched Sally walk away after returning the credit card he used to pay for lunch, leaving a note behind with her phone number and a graphic promise of a good time.

While flattered, he couldn't get the alderman's daughter off his mind. "Damn."

"What?" Meeks smirked, reading the text message he'd just received. "The lovely Ms. Sally make you an offer you can't refuse?"

"Oh, I can refuse, she's just very explicit about what she wants." Grant tossed the note in the small candle burning on the table. "Is my room clean and clear?"

"No, it's pretty infested, in fact, and they're still checking." Meeks placed his cell on his belt clip. "No worries, I got you covered."

"What the hell does that mean?" Grant slammed his fist against the table. His annoyance clear and garnered the attention of patrons seated down and across from their table.

Meeks pulled a small remote looking object from his coat pocket and handed it to Grant. "What's this?"

"That my friend is a jammer." He'd started carrying them around when he was meeting with clients and friends to make sure no one ever misconceived a conversation. "We put a larger version in your room. You'll be able to control what gets leaked and what doesn't."

"Why not just remove the damn things?"

"They don't know that they've been found," he explained. "We need to try and trace the bugs back to whoever planted them, but we can't do that unless they're active."

Grant mulled that over a few minutes "I don't like the idea of being watched, Meeks."

"My men are still checking the room, but whatever we find, we'll handle it, I promise."

"At least there is that, but—"

"Don't worry about it, man." Meeks reached for his water glass. "I told you, we got this."

A young man who appeared to be in his mid-twenties, wearing a nice but inexpensive suit, approached their table, putting both men on alert.

"Excuse me, Mr. Khambrel. My name is Mark Nadler," the man introduced, offering his hand. "I'm a community activist for the Twenty-Seventh Ward."

Meeks focused in on the man as Grant accepted his hand. "Mr. Nadler, what can I do for you?"

"It's what I hope to be able to do for you and your company," he stated giving a smile that probably was supposed to put Grant at ease but did the exact opposite.

CHAPTER 3

Autumn Knight walked into her office in the United Center, where she spent most of her days being frustrated as hell. The cream walls were littered with signed Chicago Bulls and Blackhawk championship posters, contemporary art, and feminine knickknacks that helped to tone down the masculine mahogany furnishings and sports paraphernalia. Usually, the combination had a calming effect on Autumn. Not today.

She placed her Emma Fox purse on the desk, dropped down into the leather chair, then covered her face with her hands and released a quite scream.

"You okay, boss?" Jenna Lowe, her tall, beautiful assistant appeared, looking like she should be gracing a Paris fashion runway instead of sitting behind a desk in a sports complex surrounded by concrete and wood. The flower print dress she wore made it seem more like a sunny spring day though it was raining like crazy outside.

Autumn lowered her hands, glanced up at Jenna, and smiled. "No, I'm far from okay. I don't know how I keep letting my father catch me slipping."

Jenna released an audible sigh. "What did he do now?"

"We were supposed to go to brunch this morning after some

important meeting he couldn't miss," she explained as she removed her cell from the purse before placing it in the drawer. "Instead, he took me to the hospital."

Jenna frowned and claimed a seat on the leather chair facing her desk, giving Autumn an intense scrutiny. "The hospital? Why? Are you okay?"

Autumn could hear the concern in her assistant's voice. "Yes, I'm fine. He was taking me to see Khalil Germaine."

Jenna scrunched up her face. "That's the man who owns that Castle place up in Wilmette?"

"Yes, that's the same person." Autumn shook her head, still not believing how her morning had gone. "He's also the man my father can't stand."

"Why?"

"Why can't he stand him, or, why would he take me to see him?"

Jenna adjusted her position in the chair, "Both."

"Good question. I have no clue about the latter, but, as for the former," Autumn tilted her head and shrugged. "Mr. Germaine won't do business with my father."

"Why?"

Autumn gave it some thought, "If you want to know the truth, it's because my father is a corrupt alderman and businessman, and Mr. Germaine isn't anything of the kind."

Jenna pulled out her cell and scanned the screen. "Did you eat?"

"No. I refused to play my dad's games, so I caught an Uber and came to work."

"Your calendar is clear. I'll order us some Portillo's. We can eat and talk before we tackle this afternoon's list of must do's."

"Sounds like a plan, thanks." Autumn read through the messages on her desk while Jenna placed an order for a couple of Italian beef sandwiches and fries.

"Done."

They filtered through the weekly agenda before Autumn held up one of Jenna's post-it notes that she was known for plastering all over the place and asked, "You spoke to Mr. Khambrel, and we're all set for tomorrow."

"Yep," she replied, moving to the mini refrigerator she kept in the corner of the office and pulled out two bottles of Fiji. She returned to her seat and handed a water to Autumn. "I pulled up his website, and he's very handsome. Plus, he has a panty dropping phone voice."

Autumn rolled her eyes skyward. "I could care less how he looks and sounds Jenna. I hope he's as good as all his hype."

"He has an excellent resume, and he's sexy as sin." Jenna leaned forward and lowered her voice as though she had a secret to share. "Oh yeah, did I fail to mention that he's single too?"

Autumn glanced down at Jenna's ring finger and laughed. The large diamond was hard to miss. "Aren't you a happily engaged woman?"

"Very. I've got my tall, dark, and handsome Mandingo," Jenna replied, and her whole face lit up at the mention of Jackson. "Which is why I want my gorgeous boss and friend to find love and be just as happy. Even if it's vanilla instead of chocolate."

"I don't need a man to make me happy," she declared.

"True, but they come in handy for so many of other things." Jenna swiveled her hips in the chair, leaving no doubt as to what she meant.

Both women laughed. A knock on the door snatched their attention. The young man delivering their late lunch was all smiles as he accepted the generous tip. Jenna collected their food, and they moved to the small round conference table situated on the left side of the room near the mini refrigerator. The two women spent the next forty-five minutes enjoying their lunch as Jenna brought Autumn up to speed on her wedding plans.

Jenna collected and discarded their trash. "Okay, enough about me, now spill," she said, sitting back down.

"Shortly after my father found out, from inside sources, that Mr. Germaine was in the hospital—"

"What do you mean?" Her brow crumpled.

She shook her head, then started to explain and relive the moment. Autumn thought back to the first time her father attempted to visit Mr. Germaine's and the one bright side of that trip.

Autumn watched as the driver pulled into a parking lot and then the covered garage. She sighed and turned her attention to the sixty-year-old male version of herself immaculately dressed in a gray Gevona suit.

"Father, what are we doing at the hospital? You asked me out to breakfast," she said, not trying to hide her annoyance. She was trying hard to improve her relationship with the man she knew loved her beyond reason but also saw her as that little girl who lost her mom and clung to her father being fearful of losing him too. Her taste buds were all tuned up for some Batter & Berries, and it seemed like cafeteria food is what he had in mind.

"Your work will be waiting for you when you get there, so calm down," he said, patting her on the knee like she was a petulant child. "I need you with me."

She looked up at her father while dramatically clutching a set of imaginary pearls. "The great Alderman James Knight, City Councilman, and real estate tycoon actually needs someone." She gasped and batted her eyelashes. "Needs me."

"You're my daughter, my only child, of course, I need you." *He had missed her sarcasm.* *"Too bad you don't show a little more appreciation—"*

"Let's not do this today," she snapped, instantly sobering when a constant debate seemed to be creeping into the conversation. *"You know I don't want to work in real estate. Besides, your business tactics leave a lot to be desired."* She pushed a wayward hair behind her ear and took a breath to bring about a calm she didn't feel. One of the main reasons she did not want to go into the same line of business as her father is that he had already tainted the waters to the point she couldn't even put a toe in without getting dirty.

"My business tactics gets things done," he countered with a dismissive wave. *"But enough of this nonsense."* The alderman's car door opened with the driver standing off to the side. He exited, then held out his hand. *"I need my daughter at my side while I go pay respects to one of my constituents who's been injured. It won't take long."*

Autumn heaved a sigh and grabbed her purse. *"Sure, it won't,"* she murmured, knowing that she might be at Northwestern all day. Her father was tenacious. If he thought he would gain ground and benefit by pressing an issue when another man was in a weakened state, he would do just that.

Taking her father's hand, Autumn got out the car. He gave her a once-over and smiled. *"I like your outfit."*

She glanced down at the blue pantsuit she'd paired with a white scoop neck blouse and laughed. *"Of course, you do, you bought it."*

The alderman chose to lavish expensive gifts and the occasional shopping spree on his daughter as an expression of his love. Never a real emotional connection. Always material things to make up for his *inability to express his feelings. He just expected her to know that she was loved fiercely. She expected for him to clean up his act.*

"I have excellent taste." He gestured for her to walk ahead of him, and she shook off the arrogance that came with his statement. Appearances meant everything to him. So much so that he would go out of his way to make people believe they had a close relationship, unlike when her mother was alive when they actually had been close.

Autumn headed for the glass door only to come to a quick halt. She glared at her father.

"What now, Autumn?"

The annoyance in her father's voice wasn't hard to miss.

"Why's the press here?"

He placed his palm at the small of her back and pushed her forward. "I told you, one of my more prominent constituents was injured."

Autumn stopped walking and turned towards him. "Who is this person?"

He held his daughter's gaze but remained silent.

"Father!"

"It's Khalil Germaine."

"What?"

The alderman glanced over Autumn's shoulder, and his expression closed. She noticed several photographers had them in their sights and tried to angle so she would not be easy to film.

"He was shot yesterday."

"Oh no, is he going to be okay?"

He turned her around, grabbed her elbow, and moved her forward. "I don't know. We're about to find out. Just smile and keep walking."

They maneuvered the short distance through the flashing lights and calls for comments. Autumn heard the questions still being thrown at them as they made their way into the hospital. One question, in particular, caught her attention. "Alderman Knight, has Mr. Germaine changed his mind about embracing that development plan?"

"No comment," he replied before they entered the brightly lit lobby.

"I'm a senior administrator for the hospital, Alderman Knight," a woman called out, offering a wide smile and her hand. She looked to be in her early thirties and wore a blue pleated dress that stopped above her knee, high heels that made her about the same height as Autumn, and her hair was pulled back into a tight bun that mirrored her own.

This seemed to be the go-to look for professional women these days. Autumn gave another thought to changing her style.

The way the woman's eyes roamed Autumn's father, she would soon be offering him much more—she recognized the look. James Knight, a handsome, single, rich, and powerful man, was like premium catnip to a feline.

"Yes," he replied, accepting the woman's hand and giving her that smile designed to melt a woman where she stood.

"Pleased to meet you. My name is Linda Ray. Miss Ray," she emphasized.

Autumn stepped away from her father and Miss Ray. Evidently, the two had things to discuss, and none of it included her.

She pulled out her cell phone to check messages when a sudden movement near the nurse's station caught her attention. A tall man with olive skin, a finely-trimmed beard wearing a designer suit that draped his body to perfection—he screamed strong and sexy.

He leaned in, discussing something with the nurse that seemed pretty intense. He was the most handsome man Autumn had ever seen, and his powerful presence stole her breath. The man was running his right hand through his hair shaking his head as he talked to the attentive woman.

Autumn admonished herself for staring and lusting after a man who was clearly in distress. Before she could turn away, he looked in her direction. The moment their eyes met, unfamiliar sensations flooded Autumn's body, and the oxygen in the room evaporated. She found that odd, considering they were standing in a place known to have plenty of it.

Her heart rate rapidly increased, and she was thankful to already be at the place known for handling those types of situations. With their gazes locked, Autumn gasped, and she trembled with anticipation when he took a step in her direction. Before he could close their distance, the nurse called out, and he froze. Autumn wasn't sure if she was disappointed or relieved. It should be against the law to be so sexy and masculine.

"Autumn... Autumn," her father said, placing a hand on her shoulder.

"Yes." She turned and faced him.

"Are you all right?" he asked, frowning before placing the back of his hand on her forehead. "You look a bit flushed."

"Yes, of course, I'm fine." She extracted his hand and put it back by his side. "What did you find out about Mr. Germaine?" she asked, trying to distract herself from the overwhelming feelings of desire she felt for a complete stranger. Unexpected in the fact that she was well aware that her father's protégé had been coming on strong, probably at her father's directive. She felt nothing for him whatsoever.

"He's in no condition for visitors." His voice was tinted with disappointment.

Autumn shifted her weight to one leg and placed a hand on her hip. "What's going on, father? You don't even like Mr. Germaine."

"Nothing. It doesn't matter how I feel about the man, he's a community leader who has a worldwide presence, and it's good for me to show concern."

Autumn gave her father the evil eye. "It would be good if you were actually concerned. Just as I suspected, this visit was just a farce of a publicity stunt. You were probably the one who called the press."

Jenna's laughter brought Autumn back to the present. "No offense, but your dad is something else."

"You have no idea."

"What about the guy from the hospital?"

Autumn shrugged, her mind flickering over the details of the perfect stranger. "What about him? We never met, and I'll probably never see him again."

"Too bad, he sounds hot," she said, wiggling her eyebrows.

"Whatever."

"How'd you get away this time?" Jenna's face lit up with excitement, and Autumn knew she was hoping for a more intriguing tale than the one she was about to receive.

"By the time I figured out what my father was up to, we were already at the hospital. I didn't want to be part of whatever game he was playing with Mr. Germaine, so I called an Uber and came to work. I'm sure he's still hanging around, hoping for an audience with the man."

"Like I said before." Jenna stood and stretched out her arms. "Your dad is something else."

"We should get back to work. I want to make sure everything is ready for tomorrow."

"They will be. Besides, I'd hate for you to miss out on another opportunity with a sexy, single man." Jenna winked at her friend and left the office.

Autumn closed her eyes and pictured the handsome stranger again. *That was a missed lifetime opportunity.*

CHAPTER 4

Grant met Meeks' suspicious gaze. "Excuse me, Mr. Nadler, allow me to introduce my business associate, Mr. Montgomery." Soft music echoed throughout the air of the hotel's lounge.

"Pleasure to meet you." He handed both men his business cards and gestured toward the empty chair situated between them. "May I?"

"Sure," Grant replied, switching off the ringer on his phone before placing it on his belt. "Now, how is it that you *think* you can help me, Mr. Nadler."

"Please, call me Mark."

"Okay, Mark, I'm Grant," he gestured with his head. "And he's Meeks. I'll ask again. How do you think you can help me?"

"As the winning contractor for the United Center," he began; adjusting a thin silk tie over his broad chest. "You're required to utilize a percentage of local vendors. I'm here to convince you to use a coalition of vendors in the Twenty-Seventh Ward that's not necessarily affiliated with the alderman's choice list."

Grant glanced over at Meeks before turning his attention back to Mark. "Is there a reason the vendors you're representing aren't on

Knight's list?"

The man's expression hardened, and his lips drew back in a snarl. "I'm sure there are, but the real reason is that the businesses I'm referring aren't supportive of Alderman Knight."

Meeks shifted his gaze to Grant, who gave him an imperceptible nod.

"A number of them are small, minority-owned, and can't afford to financially contribute to the alderman's keep-me-rich fund." Grant saw the younger man's jaw clench and forehead crease with concern.

Meeks' brows shot upward. "Those are pretty serious accusations."

"They're facts."

"And which one of these organizations that you're representing do you work for?" Grant asked, unable to keep the suspicion from his voice.

"None of them." He leaned forward. "Full disclosure. Up until a week ago, I was working for the alderman."

"And ..." Grant prompted.

"And what?" Mark slid forward in the chair.

Grant sighed and stared at the younger man, waiting.

Mark held the hard gaze briefly before turning his attention to Meeks, who simply titled his head, also waiting.

He held up both hands as if he was being placed under arrest. "All right, he was threatening to fire me when I quit," he reluctantly admitted.

Meeks whipped out his phone. "What's your date of birth and social security number," he asked.

Mark frowned, eyes went wide as he flickered a gaze between Grant and Meeks. "Why?"

"Because he's going to do a background check," Grant stated

before Meeks could. "Do you have a problem with that?"

They both knew that question was a sure-fire way to determine if this guy was for real or not. He could have been a plant from Knight, and they couldn't be too careful. Grant gave Meeks a pointed look and Meeks shifted his gaze to the door. Both had just made a silent bet that the young man would bolt.

"No," he replied, squaring his shoulders and presenting his chin before reaching into his pocket. He pulled out his wallet and handed his driver's license and rattled of the social security number to Meeks. "Use whatever you need. I was born and raised right here in Chicago, Lincoln Park."

Grant gave the younger man a half-smile. *Impressive.*

Meeks took pictures of each object before handing everything back. As Meeks went about his business, Grant turned his attention back to Mark. "Want a drink?"

"Yes, thanks."

"Beer?"

Mark tucked the wallet back in his pocket. "Sure."

Grant raised an index finger, getting Sally's attention. Her whole face lit up and she exaggerated her hip movements on the way over. Obviously, his simple action made her entertain the wrong idea. He was not in the habit of randomly picking up overly aggressive women. The women he'd been with were just as busy and career focused as Grant. Short-term, no strings affairs were expected and accepted.

"Change your mind, handsome?" She gifted him with a wide smile and winked. "Have you figured out what *else* I can get you?"

"Three beers, whatever's on tap."

She scowled, then spoke barely above a whisper. "That's it?"

Grant smiled up at Sally and nodded. "That's it."

She released an audible sigh, turned, trudged towards the bar and said something to the blond spiked-haired man wielding a silver shaker.

"Now tell us why he fired you." After checking his phone, Meeks placed it facedown near the salt and pepper containers and gave Mark his undivided attention.

"Well, I have to start with when I graduated—"

"Where did you attend school?" Grant asked.

"UIC, I have a graduate degree in urban planning," Mark proudly proclaimed.

"The University of Illinois?" Meeks noted, keying something in his cell. "Means you stayed close to home."

"I wanted to be here for my grandmother. Plus, I wanted to work for my community. I was hired by the alderman's right-hand man, Richmond Kane."

"Yes, we met him this morning," Grant acknowledged with a look at Meeks.

Mark shook his head. "Richmond is a smart and driven man who's worshiping at the feet of a criminal."

Meeks held up a hand to halt the conversation as Sally approached with their orders and placed one in front of each man. "Shall I keep the tab open?"

"Sure, why not, and thanks."

Sally gave Grant a dismissive nod and walked away.

Grant caught Meeks smirk as he tasted the brew.

"That's the second time you insinuated that the alderman is a criminal in some way," Meeks said.

Mark also took a sip from his glass, his dark eyes shifting to focus on the two sets of eyes that bored into him intensely. "Because it's true. People in the community talked about the alderman like he was some Godfather. There's some truth to the fact that he did a lot of great things for the community, but he made sure to line his own pockets in the process."

"How do you mean?" Grant asked, fingering the bottom of the icy mug.

"For years our neighborhood went through gentrification, the alderman convinced my grandmother to sell her place to him below market value. She owned a three-story apartment building for thirty years that was in a premium location. The ground level housed a few businesses; one was her bakery. He told her that the renovation required to bring her up to code would be too expensive." He reached for his water and Grant knew he was trying to cool down. Anger was written all over his face and in his posture.

Mark sighed before continuing. "He failed to mention all the government subsidies available to help with those renovations. And to hide his double-dealing, the good alderman allowed my grandmother to run her bakery rent-free as long as she agreed to become one of his preferred vendors."

"Preferred vendor?" Grant echoed.

"Means whenever he needed something like baked goods for events, he'd get her to provide it."

"For free?" Meeks asks, his face contorted by anger.

"No, but it might as well have been," Mark replied, "My grandmother never exceeded a profit margin over sixty percent. Because the alderman wasn't charging her rent for the bakery or her apartment, she never thought anything was wrong."

"Damn." Grant finished off his beer and shared a worried glance with Meeks who was well aware of the illegal maneuver and exactly how vulnerable Mark's grandmother was.

"Yeah, because what she didn't know was that while he was ingratiating himself with all these businesses by getting them better rates for services they would never have received on their own, he was charging the clients a finder's fee," Mark added as he finished his beer.

Meeks sat up in her chair. "Can you prove any of this?"

"Even if I could, it'll do no good. The people around here think he's a God. Especially when he became associated with the Castle."

"The Castle?" Grant slid forward in his chair. "Why?"

"The place was a playground for the wealthy and powerful, and the majority of his contributors. It led to a lot of new business. It kept my grandmother and several others in the community busy making good money, or so they thought."

"What does that mean?" Grant asked, ignoring a patron who passed by a little too close trying to get his attention.

"That's when everyone started making about seventy-five cents on the dollar. Of course, the alderman made the other twenty-five cents from their hard work."

"And if anyone complained?" Meeks prompted, frowning.

"That's just it. No one did. That's because everyone was making money. Everyone was happy," then he grimaced. "That is, until the bottom fell out and the gravy train ran off the tracks."

CHAPTER 5

Autumn read through the architect and construction contract for the third time. She had to make sure she knew everything about what was expected of Grant Khambrel. She was making notes when her door opened.

"I know Jenna, it's after six," she said without looking up from the documents. "And I'll be leaving shortly."

"That's good to hear, but it's not Jenna," the familiar strong male voice stated.

"Richmond." Autumn murmured before raising her head to stare into the handsome face of a man she'd known most of her adult life. She'd always found Richmond attractive, but his ambition and willingness to skirt the line between right and wrong was too much like her father. That fact alone made his desire for them to explore a romantic relationship a nonstarter. Unfortunately, he was having a hard time getting that memo.

"Hello, beautiful," he greeted, leaning onto the door jam.

"What are you doing here?" She asked, putting the paperwork aside and focusing on him. Today, he wore an expensive gray pinstriped suit, looking more like her father than ever.

"I came to take my favorite girl to dinner." He pushed off the door and walked further into her office. "Better yet, why don't you let me fire up my grill and make us a couple of steaks?"

She gave him a dirty look. "I'm not your girl, Richmond."

"Excuse me, Autumn. Do you need anything before I take off?" Jenna entered the room carrying a large white binder labeled B&G Construction and handed it over. She noticed their guest leaning against conference table. "Richmond…"

"Jenna…"

Autumn bit her bottom lip to keep the laugh from escaping her mouth. Jenna couldn't care a rat's ass for Richmond. She merely tolerated him for Autumn's sake. For reasons she never chose to share, Jenna didn't think Richmond was good enough for her friend, and that gave Autumn pause on top of her own misgivings. She was not going to trade her father for a carbon copy. The man she would consider a life-mate, at least needed to have his ethics and morals intact.

"No, this is all I need, thanks," Autumn said. "And you can take off."

Jenna glanced over her shoulder putting green eyes on Richmond who was staring at Autumn as though she was the only meal he would have today. He licked his lips in the same manner of a wolf before he attacked his pray. Jenna turned her attention back to Autumn and asked, "You sure?"

"I'm sure," she said, standing, offering what she hoped was a reassuring smile. "I'll be leaving soon. I have homework to do."

Both women glanced at the large binder.

"You're ready, there's nothing that B&G will be able to pull over your eyes," Jenna reassured.

Autumn came from around the desk, shooing her toward the door.

"Thanks, now go home and enjoy that wonderful fiancé of yours."

"I will." Jenna pulled Autumn into a hug and whispered in her ear, "You still got your taser in your bag, right?"

Autumn threw her head back and laughed. "Yes."

"See you tomorrow," she said, sauntering out the door but not without putting a warning look in Richmond's direction. He returned her look with a smile that reminded Autumn of her father's public face.

"Now, like I said … how about you coming over to my place so we can enjoy each other," Richmond offered, moving to stand in front of Autumn, then placing his hands on her arms.

"Thanks for the invitation, but as you can see," she gestured to the desk littered with binders and open folders. "I have a ton of work to get through before meeting with the architect and construction company renovating this place."

"I'm sure you're more than prepared. It's not in your nature not to be." He smirked. "Besides, I don't anticipate any problems with those folks."

Autumn recognized that look, and an alarm went off in her head. She stepped out of his hold, crossed her arms at her chest, and frowned. Another company that was in her father's pocket? Damn! She couldn't seem to stay off the radar of their underhanded dealings no matter how hard she tried.

"So how much money are you and my father making off *this* deal?"

Richmond's face lit up in the kind of delight he shouldn't be anywhere close to feeling as he laughed. "You're always so suspicious of us." He raised his right hand and used the tips of his fingers to smooth out the worry lines stretched across her forehead.

"And I have reason to be." Autumn moved back to her desk and gathered up her things. "A new company comes to town and they're about to make millions renovating this place. Then you drop the hint that they won't be a problem." She glared at Richmond, who didn't seem bothered. "There is no way in hell you can expect me to believe my father doesn't have his hooks into this contract somehow."

"Autumn, sweetheart—"

"Don't sweetheart me, Richmond," she snapped, fisting her hands at her sides. "Just tell me the truth for once."

Richmond sighed and shoved his hands in his pockets. "The alderman doesn't have his fingers in *every* new company that comes into Chicago to do business, Autumn."

She placed her hands on her hips. "Since when Richmond? We both know my father doesn't do anything for anyone unless he benefits in some way. That's been his deal since he took office." Autumn reached over to shut down her computer the moment Richmond tried to peek at the screen. "And I notice you didn't specifically mention that he didn't have his hands in the company I'm speaking of."

"You didn't ask—specifically."

"I shouldn't have to," she shot back, totally taken aback that he was double-talking around the issue.

Richmond shrugged. "What's wrong with taking care of yourself in the process of taking care of the community? Mr. Knight makes sure he—and his family—well taken care of, too." He raised his left eyebrow and gave her an accusatory look. "Last time I checked, Autumn, you received a first-class education and were able to travel the world thanks your father's hard work."

"*His* hard work?" Autumn snarled at Richmond.

"Damn right." His eyes narrowed to slits. "I've worked side-by-side with the man for years, and his only motive has been to make his community a better place to live and provide a good life for his family. I don't see anything wrong with that."

"There isn't, if he's open and honest about it," her voice raised, and she pointed her index finger at his chest. "Which we both know he's not."

"You don't know that, and I certainly don't know that to be true." He pushed out an audible sigh, and his eyes softened. "Look, I didn't come here to discuss business and certainly not to talk about your complicated relationship with your father. Why don't—"

She held up a hand to halt anything else. "My relationship with my father is none of your business, and I'd like to thank you to keep your opinions to yourself, Richmond,"

He held her angry glare for a moment. "Look, I don't want to argue with you. Why don't we get out of here, go back to my place—"

Autumn's defiant stare stopped Richmond midsentence.

"Okay, how about I take you to that little Italian spot you love so much."

She closed her eyes and took a deep breath, trying to calm her rapidly beating heart. Autumn slowly raised her lids, and Richmond's brown eyes bored into her. Trying to ignore him, she opened her desk drawer and removed her purse. Autumn was angry at herself for letting Richmond get under her skin. He was right; her relationship with her father was complicated and what bothered her the most was that it shouldn't be.

Autumn had been the apple of her parents' eyes. James and Tina Knight grew up on the south side of Chicago and worked hard to care for their only child and do right by their community. Tina Knight, an elementary school teacher, taught in the public-school system while

James used his skill as a defense attorney to help the people in his neighborhood, including the questionable clients that most attorneys turned away.

When Tina was caught in the crossfire of a gang war and was killed, losing the love of his life was the catastrophic event that forever changed James. He shifted his career focus and moved his then seven-year-old traumatized daughter to Lincoln Park. As a father, his only priority was to ensure his child would be safe and wants for nothing. It wasn't until after Autumn graduated from college that she learned her father, now an elected member of the City Council, wasn't a straightforward businessman that her mother would have been proud of.

Richmond checked his watch. "Come on, Autumn. You have to eat."

"Dinner, that's it."

"Yes, ma'am." He raised his hands to indicate he would keep them to himself.

Autumn grabbed her things and thought about a way she could milk him for a little intel on B&G. "And no more talk about my father. I'm serious. Break my rule, and I'll get my food to go," she promised.

Richmond laughed and said, "That wouldn't be the first time."

"But it *will* be the last."

CHAPTER 6

Grant's brows drew together. "What do you mean the bottom fell out Mark?"

Meeks had an idea about what he meant, but he wanted confirmation.

"According to my grandmother," Mark replied. "The once upscale and conscious-minded group of people—an older, more refined clientele that frequented the Castle, changed. An even more rich, wilder and politically connected group of people started hanging out in the place."

"I see," Grant replied, gritting his teeth.

Mark ran both hands down his face and released a frustrated sigh. "The new crowd wanted a different type of entertainment, and their appetites called for goods and service that those in our community couldn't satisfy." His nostrils flared and a grimace followed. "Those who were running the place used their own people to satisfy those specific requirements."

"They stopped using the alderman's people," Meeks concluded with a look toward Grant who nodded since he definitely understood where this story was headed.

"Yep, so the good alderman came back to the community he

claimed to want to help and started putting the screws to them all over again." Mark fisted his hands at his side. "The only person he cared about was his daughter, Autumn."

Grant's breath caught, and he felt like the wind had been knocked out of his chest at the mention of the woman's name. Whatever was going on with him, he had to get it under control. Such an intense reaction to a woman he'd never officially met wasn't something he wanted, ever. But he still needed to know how deep she was into things where her father was concerned. And did she have an unethical tendency of her own?

"Is she involved with any of his businesses?" Meeks asked, acknowledging the woman flirtatiously waving as she passed their table, with a quick appreciative nod.

"Not that I've heard, but I don't know her like that," Mark answered. "What I've heard is that she's Knight's pride and joy and has always been his number one priority."

"Here you go, gentlemen." Sally handed each man another glass of beer and filled their coffee cups. Can I get you anything to eat?"

"No, we're good, thanks," Grant replied, noticing how the place had begun to fill up with the after-work crowd.

Meeks bypassed the beer and took a drink from his coffee cup. "What did you mean by putting the screws to them?"

"Those on his preferred list now only make about a forty-five percent profit for their hard work," Mark answered, silencing his ringing phone before reaching for the beer.

"When did you find out about all this?" Grant questioned, sliding his mug toward the center of the table.

"The summer before my senior year when I interned for another alderman. I asked my grandmother about what I'd heard, and she confirmed it. Only in her mind, Alderman Knight was still helping the community. She felt it was only right that he got paid for his years of service."

"So, his double-dealings, is that why you quit?" Meeks asked, adjusting so he had a better angle to see the front entrance.

"Sadly, no," Mark admitted. He lowered his eyes briefly, taking in a calming breath before meeting both men's hard looks. "In spite of everything, my grandmother made a good living. She put me through school and since retiring she's been traveling the world with her best friend."

"That's good, right?" Grant asked noticing his somber look.

"Yeah, it is good, but she could have, hell should have, made so much more. When Raymond recruited me, I thought," he ran his hand through his hair and sighed. "I could try to change things from the inside."

"How'd that work out for you?" Meeks asked, sarcasm all in his tone and dour expression.

"It didn't," he confessed. "Whenever I tried to get Knight to reach out to other parts of the city or at least work on other projects with different aldermen, I got shut down. He didn't want any of them in his affairs. At least not the way he was into theirs."

Grant nodded his understanding. "What was it that finally made you say, I'm out?"

"When I brought my list of vendors who I thought he should consider presenting for the United Center project. Richmond, who now has more power in that office, told me to drop it and get with the program or else. That's when I resigned."

Grant rubbed his hands together before intertwining his fingers. "So now what, you're looking for a job?"

Mark raised his chin. "No, I'm looking to help my community the right way."

"Well, how do you make your living?" Meeks questioned. His gaze narrowed with suspicion.

Mark's shoulders dropped. "I was raised here, but I was born in New York. My father died on 9/11. He was a firefighter."

Grant saw how the young man's chest fell, and his eyes filled with sadness. "I'm sorry for your loss."

"Me too, man," Meeks echoed.

"Thanks for that." Mark put his hand on the mug but didn't make a move to take another drink. "My mom couldn't handle it, so she sent me here to be with my grandmother—I was four at the time."

"Why?" Grant ran his left hand under his chin—realizing he needed a shave and would be sure to get it done before his meeting with Autumn. But knowing who Mark Nadler was would go a long way to having a little bit of intelligence on the alderman.

He lifted his glass and finished off his drink. "She killed herself."

"Damn," both men chorused.

"Anyway, I got money from the 9/11 fund, and my grandmother put it in a trust for me. In spite of having all that cash on hand, she paid for my education. She said that money wasn't hers to spend. It was for my future and that I was her responsibility. I owe her everything."

Grant thought of the healthy trust fund his uncle had started with the proceeds from the sale of his family's assets and also life insurance policies that he never touched, even to this day. He also thought raising his nephew was his responsibility and the sacrifices the man made to ensure Grant lived in a comfortable and safe environment was profound. "I like the way your grandmother thinks," Grant complimented.

"Me too," Mark said with a smile that lit his eyes. And in that one move, his whole demeanor improved. "Like I said, I'm not looking for anything in return. I would like for you to consider using some, if not all, of these vendors because they should have been the only ones on that list in the first place." He pulled out a document and handed it to Grant.

He scanned the number of names. "This is quite a list."

"Yes, it is," Mark said, tapping an index finger against his knee. "This community has a number of small businesses capable of providing superior service."

Grant handed it over to Meeks. "If they check out, I might be able to find something for a number of them. That's if they check out."

"They will," Mark reassured, then stood to gather his things. "I've taken up enough of your—"

"Before you go." Grant could feel Meeks' questioning glare. "I could use your help."

Mark dropped back down in the chair. "My help, how?"

"I need someone on my team who knows the city and the players," he answered. "As you know, the United Center renovation and expansion is at least a three-year project."

"Someone who can prevent us from stepping on any landmines," Meeks murmured, looking away as if he was thinking out loud.

"Landmines, huh?"

"Just give it some thought." Grant pulled out one of his business cards and handed it to him. "Not that it's a priority to you, but I pay well."

"Let us do our due diligence. We'll talk in a couple of days about the vendors you're recommending," Meeks promised.

The three men stood and shook hands. "I look forward to it, and thanks for hearing me out." Mark maneuvered past a group of women who'd clearly come to party as they invited him to join them before he politely refused then was out of the revolving door of the lounge.

"That was an interesting turn of events," Grant stated as he signed the bar bill.

Meeks checked his watch. "Let's get upstairs. Jed's waiting, and I have a plane to catch."

"Did he find anything?"

Meeks leaned back in the chair and raised his glass in a toast. "Yes, and we're going to make them work for us."

CHAPTER 7

Grant's cell vibrated as they stood in the lobby waiting at the bank of elevators. "Give me a second, Meeks. I need to take this." He slid the screen and took the call. "Jai, what's going on, my man?"

Meeks put his back against the wall waiting for the elevator to arrive.

"I heard you were in Chicago and need to know if you could slide through for a hot minute," Jai said. "Need you to meet with the Knights. We'd like to put an offer on the table."

"Business offer?" Grant questioned.

"The best kind," Jai shot back.

"What time?"

"Tomorrow morning. How about seven-thirty?"

Grant took in a breath. "I have a meeting at eight-thirty, that'll be cutting it pretty close."

"Can we come to you?"

Grant signaled to Meeks and asked, "Jai and the Knights want to take a meeting here."

"Not a good idea," Meeks said.

"Shoot me the address and I'll come to you, but I'm going to need to slide through earlier than seven-thirty though. I heard Chicago traffic can be a beast, even in short distances. How's six-thirty?" Grant figured it wouldn't be a problem since most of his friends were early risers.

"Sounds like a plan."

Grant disconnected the call.

"What's that about," Meeks asked on their ascent in the elevator.

"Set foot in Chicago and business is coming out of the woodwork."

"Architect humor, he teased."

"Well, you know. I get it honest."

Grant walked into his suite overlooking the city skyline to find a tall, burly man standing in the middle of the living room holding a conversation on a cell. Fluent in several languages, Grant couldn't help but hear the man converse in Italian explaining to someone he was calling "sweetheart" how much he did appreciate all she did for him, in the kitchen, as well as the bedroom, but he might be late tonight.

Tuning the man out, Grant turned his attention to Meeks. "What's going on?"

Before Meeks could respond, the man ended his call, turned and offered his hand. "Good afternoon Mr. Khambrel, Jed Shield."

"Good afternoon, Mr. Shield." Grant shook the man's massive hand but sent a questioning glare toward Meeks.

"We good?" Meeks asked Jed.

"Yep, all clear," he assured, handing Meeks a small black object that looked more like a remote control than what he could only assume was a device that controlled his privacy. Almost like the one that Meeks' had given him earlier.

"What's up, Meeks?" Grant insisted

Meeks held up the device that had buttons, switches and a blinking green light. He nodded to Jed. "Mr. Khambrel, we—"

"It's Grant."

"And I'm Jed," he said, gesturing toward several objects in the room. "We found three additional bugs in the living room area, two in the bedroom, and a video camera hidden in the bedroom vent, all voice-activated."

"Damn it." Grant punched his right fist in the palm of his left hand. "A video recorder in the bedroom. What in the hell is going on?" His gaze bounced between Meeks and Jed not expecting a real answer. They were just as dumbfounded as he was.

"We're not sure the bugs were specifically meant for you," Meeks admitted with a raised eyebrow.

"What the hell does that mean?"

"We checked the other executive suites. The ones used specifically for VIPs and found the same set up," Jed explained.

"What?" Grant didn't know if that was a good thing, or if things had just gotten worse.

All three men took a seat around the coffee table. "Jed is retired FBI and worked in the Chicago office for fifteen years. He remembered a case from a few years ago where high-rise apartments were bugged," Meeks said, his jaw set in a hard line. "And if anything noteworthy were discovered, the owners were blackmailed."

Grant sank further into the sofa. "And you think that's what's happening here? Blackmail?" He thought back to the note he'd received before he left Texas. Grant didn't know if his situation could be connected to whatever might be going on at the hotel.

"We'll know when we pull the guest list from the last six months and have a conversation with those folks," Meeks explained. "We need to find out if they paid more than their room rate."

"I assume that gadget in your hand is what's allowing us to speak so freely," Grant said. "And it's different from the one you gave me before. That one for portable purposes?"

"That would be correct," Meeks confirmed with a gesture that the encompassed the room. "It's jamming all signals coming in and out of the room, including our cell phones, so let's speed this up. I have a family to get back to."

Grant ran his hand down his face then sat forward, resting his elbows on his knees. "What now?"

"We leave the bugs live and in place." Jed smiled and rubbed his hands together as if he was about to grab hold of something delicious. "When you want to speak freely, flip the switch."

Meeks handed Grant the controller.

"In the meantime, my guys will work on tracing the signal," Jed said, his shoulders pushed back, and chin raised confidently. "Once we truly know what we're dealing with, we can see if this has anything to do with Knight, or *another* set of criminals we don't know about."

Grant jerked his head towards Meeks so fast he felt dizzy. Didn't he specifically say they would keep that part of the investigation between them?

Meeks held up both hands, stopping the onslaught of profanity he knew was coming. "Before you lose it, listen to me. We need help looking into James Knight man, and this is Jed's city. He has the expertise and connections we need. You trusted me to help. This is me helping, so let me."

"I'm very good at what I do," Jed promised, giving Grant his full attention. "I'll root out whoever's behind all this, and while we do things differently in Chicago, we'll resolve things in any way you like."

Meeks shook his head. "We will handle things the right way, trust me."

"I do trust you, Meeks. What about the video camera in the bedroom?" He shook his head. "I'm not thrilled about someone watching me sleep. Suppose I do something I don't want anyone to see."

"We pretty much disabled it," Meeks smirked. "Jed."

"I placed a dead bug on the lens." Seeing the confused look on Grant's face and guessing his next question, Jed continued. "We want whoever put it up there to come check it out, and we'll catch their image on our camera's. Then we can run it through facial recognition software."

"Your cameras? As in there's more than one?" Grant frowned and stood, the others followed suit.

"Yes, we added one in the bedroom and two in the living area."

Grant placed his hands in his pockets. "Why?"

"We want to see who comes in and out of here."

Autumn's face popped in Grant's head. Suppose … He took his right hand and rubbed the back of his neck, trying to ease the tension. "About the bedroom camera…"

Jed offered Grant a knowing smile. "We got you. If, for some reason, you need privacy in the bedroom." He pointed at the control. "Push the button on the upper left, and it'll turn off the cameras. There's only one in there."

Grant tossed the controller up in the air and caught it, feeling how lightweight it was. "So, this thing controls my privacy."

"Pretty much. Remember, when the jammer is on, it knocks out all signals. Keep it off as much as possible, so no one suspects anything." Jed checked his watch and then moved toward the door.

"I have to head out. My wife will have my ass if I'm late for dinner."

Grant grinned, remembering the conversation he'd overheard when he walked into the hotel room. "Look, you both should head out." He perched on the arm of the sofa. "I hate this. I feel like I should change hotels. Better still, I think I'll buy a place."

Jed gave him an appreciative nod. "You got it like that, huh?"

"I'll text you Kayla Devine's contact information," Meeks promised pulling out his phone. "She's the realtor Francine used to find our office."

Jed smiled from his spot at the door and said, "I know Kayla. She's really good and very beautiful."

I guess he does know a lot of people. Autumn's image filled his mind again, and while he had no intention of giving his thought wings, the words were out of his mouth before he could stop them. "Do you know Alderman Knight's daughter?"

He tried to brace himself for his body's response to her name flowing past his lips, but he knew it wouldn't help. Meeks put a disapproving look on his at the same time an eyebrow winged upward.

"Autumn Knight, of course." Jed walked back in, stopping when he made it to the center of the room. "She's nothing like her father and is exceptionally beautiful as well."

Grant frowned. For some unknown reason, the man's innocent compliment annoyed the hell out of him. "You are married right?"

"Happily, but I'm also Italian," he said, laughing. "Noticing beautiful women is a God-given right."

"On that note," Meeks headed for the door and Jed was on his heels. "We'll talk tomorrow."

Thinking about the beautiful woman he would come face-to-face with soon, had his body hard and aching. He knew of only one way to remedy that feeling. Well, one way to do it alone. He walked into the bedroom, opened the drawer and pulled out his workout clothes. Aware of the cameras, Grant went to change in the bathroom. No sense giving whoever was watching an eyeful of the goods.

Dressed and ready ten minutes later, Grant grabbed his phone and headed for the gym. He planned to push himself to exhaustion, grab a quick bite to eat, and call it a night. Tomorrow he would finally meet the woman who'd been invading his dreams like an enemy would a foreign country. He reached for the doorknob when his cell vibrated. The call was coming from a blocked number.

"Grant Khambrel."

"Welcome to Chicago," a voice welcomed on the other end. "I assume the meeting with Alderman Knight went well. Do as you're told and keep your contract and that stellar reputation you covet so much." The caller laughed before the phone went dead.

Grant looked at the phone and whispered, *"Damn."*

CHAPTER 8

"Good morning boss," Jenna greeted, entering Autumn's office wearing a green print dress that fell above her knee and sexy high heels increasing her petite frame by another five inches. She was holding a clipboard and a coffee mug. "Here you go."

"Thanks," she said, her eyes roaming her friend before accepting the coffee cup. "What are you doing here so early? You're not due in for another hour." She placed the Best Boss mug on the desk. "And why are you wearing those heels, hot date?"

"I know how you get at the start of a new project," Jenna said, laughing. "It's like the first day of school."

"And…" she prompted, raising her cup to her lips.

"And," Jenna shrugged. "I felt like dressing up. With all the construction planned, after today it'll be jeans, running shoes, and flats."

Autumn took a sip of her coffee, kept her gaze on her assistant, feeling the lie for exactly what it was. "Whatever. Since you're here, you might as well make yourself useful." She gestured toward the stack of papers sitting in her outbox.

"Sure, but first," she plopped down in the chair facing the desk. "I have some tea."

Tea, girl? Call it what it is, you love to gossip.

Autumn was amazed how easily Jenna could switch between professional assistant to good girlfriend. She checked her watch. "Mr. Khambrel will be here in forty-five minutes. I don't have time for this Jenna."

"Sure, you do, especially since it's about Mr. Sexy Man himself," she declared, wiggling her eyebrows.

Autumn took another drink and focused on Jenna over the rim of her cup. "Fine, five minutes."

Jenna clasped her hands, trying to contain her excitement. "Rumor has it he's one of those Kings. You know, the ones running that beautiful Castle."

Now that was news. Autumn slid forward in her chair. "How do you know that?"

"You remember my friend Karen, the tall thin blond who used to be a Victoria's Secret model? We went to brunch with her and also a few of her friends last month."

"And?" Autumn picked up her pen flicked it between her fingers, a nervous habit from grammar school that she'd never been successful in breaking.

"Well, her sister's best friend's brother just got hired on as part of the new security team."

After her father's failed attempt at trying to speak with the big man himself, she'd asked Lola Samuels, a member of their publicity outfits, to pull as much information she could on the Castle. Lola came through big time. What she found about the Castle's purpose was endearing, but the reports coming from that place ever since Khalil Germaine had gone on a world tour, were disturbing. The fact that her father had his hands in anything related to the Castle meant she was certain that there was some dirt that he had thrown into the mix. But how? And why?

Further digging pulled up stock certificates and corporation papers that had been filed recently. Then she also found that Grant Khambrel was involved. And research on all nine of the men showed that they each brought something dynamic to the table. How on earth were these men going to wrest control from men like her father who were intent on holding onto whatever power they still held.

"Wait," Autumn said, finally processing the statement Jenna had just made. "I thought the Donner Group handled the security for the Castle?"

"Not anymore. The Donner Group are the ones handling security here on event nights, right?" Jenna asked, eyeing Autumn curiously.

"Yes, they're one of my father's preferred clients. Have been for years."

Jenna's brows snapped together, and her head tilted. "Preferred client?"

"Never mind." Autumn gave a dismissive wave.

"Well, it seems the new Kings of the Castle have cleaned house."

Now that certainly sounds promising.

"There's a whole new team running the place, and Grant Khambrel—and didn't I say he's single and sexy as sin—is one of them."

"Well, good for him." Autumn put her pen down, deciding it wasn't best to let her assistant know that what she had presented wasn't gossip or news for that matter. She always made it her business to stay ahead of the curve. Her father made that a common occurrence, which is why she was still upset about the blindside that happened at Northwestern. From what she had learned from Lola,

Autumn had been spot on.

There had been a media blackout on that shooting which had taken place on the Castle grounds. Somehow her father's informants had tipped him off to what happened, and he called in the press despite the fact that Khalil Germaine and his son, Vikkas, had wanted the Wilmette Police to handle the investigation discreetly. What her father had to gain from publicizing the tragic set of events was beyond even Autumn's understanding.

"All right, so you filled me in," she said to Jenna. "Now can we get to work? Is everything ready?"

Jenna stood and handed Autumn the clipboard. "Absolutely. The question is, are you ready?" She gave her friend a suggestive smile.

* * *

Grant exited the elevator and was making his way through the hotel's lobby to his waiting car, when he spotted a beautiful woman with a wide smile wearing a gray dress with heels that accentuated a pair of long legs, approaching. She had *Chicago Tribune* credentials hanging around her neck and the Hotel concierge on her heels.

"Good morning, Mr. Khambrel—"

"Excuse me Miss, I told you to wait outside. You can't accost our guest," the concierge called out. He looked across the lobby to another employee and said, "Call security."

"Mr. Khambrel, my name is Lindsey Newton and I'm a reporter for the Chicago Trib."

He gestured to the badge she wore, "I can see that."

"My apologies, Mr. Khambrel. I told her she wasn't allowed to approach you, or any of our guests for that matter, in this way."

"I understand you're one of the new owners of that Castle. I hear they call you the King of Lincoln Park, why is that?" The red lips slanted upward. "I just need ten minutes, Mr. Khambrel," she implored.

Grant wasn't sure how widespread knowledge of their takeover had gotten. While he hated orchestrated publicity, Grant knew if he wanted to maintain some level of privacy, it was a necessity. He never took interviews on the fly, but considering how much this woman already knew, he didn't think it was too bad of an idea—for a few minutes at least anyway.

"It's okay, Bob," he said to the concierge reading his name badge. He turned his attention to the pleading woman standing in front of him. "I'll give you until I reach my car."

They started walking at the same time Bob glared at her and stormed away. "Why do you call yourselves Kings?" She presented her phone which she was using as a recording device.

"Short answer, we are men who hold chief authority over the property known as The Castle. Next…"

"Why are you called King of Lincoln Park?"

"It's where I was raised since the age of ten," he replied stepping out of the hotel's door.

"You won the United Center contract and I hear you're working on updating the Castle too. How do you handle it all?"

"I have a great team and I'm good at multi-tasking." Grant greeted his driver with a nod as he stood holding the door open.

That was painless.

"Are you seeing anyone?" She asked in a hushed tone.

Grant sighed and stopped his progress. *Spoke too soon.* The interview had taken an inappropriate turn and that was disappointing.

"It was nice meeting you, Miss Newton." He moved to step in the car.

"There's a rumor that someone is coming for The Castle," she yelled out. "You might want to know who they are."

Grant looked over his shoulders and said, "You should know better than to listen to rumors. Have a nice day." He got in the car and signed for the driver to close the door.

That's why you don't do impromptu interviews.

CHAPTER 9

"A new rehabilitation center, that's the business deal you wanted to discuss," Grant asked, glancing around the room looking into the faces of the men he considered family.

"This one will be dedicated to health and fitness," Jai said to Grant as Hiram settled into the chair beside them. "And later, based on a proposal from my wife's former nurse, and my new employee, we'll build another one focused on the first five years of an at-risk child's life. But first, this one."

"What do you mean?" Grant asked, gesturing for the rest of the Knights, Vikkas, Daron, Kaleb, Dwayne, Alejandro, Shaz, and Mariano to have a seat. The Knights were employees of Jai's health center who were being mentored by the Kings so they, too, could take on some of the issues that plagued their communities.

"Your centers have been focused on rehabilitation. Even the one on the Castle grounds is focused on ground-breaking treatments. Why the diversion into something outside of your norm?"

"Because I want to tackle the issue of how weight and other illnesses can be related to childhood trauma and not just genetics," Jai said with a pointed look at the men around the table.

"That's admirable, but there are already a number of fitness centers around the country," Grant said, fighting to keep the concern from his voice.

"Not like this one," Hiram said, and Falcon nodded. "First we get folks moving through dance. Feeling good. Aqua aerobics and sports. Hot Hula Fitness, Chicago Style Stepping, Salsa, Yoga, Massages. Same things we do at Chetan, but this time, it's for folks who don't have the issues that our patients do."

"We look at how a person became obese—from the womb, genetics, blood type, other factors," Ryan said. "We're looking for causation, not just pushing back from the table or turning down a meal."

"Or fad diets," Shaz added, frowning like the idea of such a thing made him ill. "A body in motion, stays in motion."

"We're applying the same principles that Jai had for Chetan to Maisha."

"Maisha? Is that a woman?" Grant questioned, making notes in his phone.

"No, it's the name of the center. Maisha NZuri. Means life is good in Swahili. Maisha will suffice, because it means life," Hiram said. The corners of his mouth turned up. "And that's something that we're trying to give people who have been ridiculed, made to feel deficient instead of completely understood. We give them those healthy options, including having access to better food choices."

"But that fitness component," Shaz grinned. "That's boss. Everyone deserves a chance at a healthy life."

Jai sat back in the chair, allowing his employees to take a front seat. Grant could see the pride beaming off him. These men, who were former guests of the Illinois penal system, had shaken off a great deal of their pasts, and were running like hell toward the brightest of futures.

"Tell me how you seeing this is working," Grant said, though he really didn't need to know. He merely wanted to see how much thought the Knights had put into it before approaching him to build a set of facilities that would help them accomplish a monumental feat. Yes, weight loss and fitness were all the craze, but keeping people motivated for a longer period would be the major issue.

"We'll have a team of therapists on staff—chosen by this woman right here." He tapped a finger on the edge of a photo that accompanied Sesvalah's curriculum vitae. "She uses unconventional methods to achieve healing. Her process works on the whole person—mind, body, and spirit, and not focused on dosing people up with pills to mask the issues. If there is a need for it yes, but that's not her go-to as part of her practice."

"And you know this because ..."

"All of us have had sessions with her as part of working at Chetan," Michael said. "We didn't know how much our pasts had to do with our choices."

"Or how being in prison could create inner trauma as well," Falcon added. "Mental health isn't taken seriously in the Black community until something horrible happens. I like that she focuses on us taking ownership of the things we did and weighing out choices in the future."

Grant absorbed that, and how close that statement came to his current dilemma. Unfortunately for him, it wasn't all his doing. Unraveling the choices his uncle made in the past was presenting the type of challenges that had a direct impact on his future.

All the men were watching him closely, Jai especially, then he said, "So what are your misgivings about this?"

Grant shrugged, pushing his own issues aside. "But won't that religion thing get in the way? She's a pastor, right? Folks already feeling some kind of way when it comes to that."

"The reason I chose Sesvalah," Hiram said, tapping the edge of the table and standing, "Is because she is versed on the art of therapy without infusing spiritual guilt and things that weigh her patients down. She is well learned in several religions, just like Khalil, which makes her the best person to relate to people of all ethnic backgrounds."

Jai lowered his gaze to the floor, but his smile was hard to miss. Though Grant originally had misgivings about bringing the Knights in under the wings of the Kings, that had to be one of the best things that Jai had done. The Knights were soaking up everything faster than the Kings could lay it down.

"We'll even be in line for some government grants," Jai said proudly.

"On that I disagree," Grant said. "You don't want none of those people all up in your business. Ask me how I know."

"Word," Hiram added. "Fundraisers can help cover the costs of classes and treatments. We start small, then grow according to what the center's budget can handle. But building the space to be energy efficient, solar panels and all that, means shaving off costs on the back end."

"Word," Grant said, causing everyone else to laugh. "I can cover you on that. Building those types of structures has been a specialty of mine for a long time."

"We have a center dedicated to healing those hanging between life and death, why not a center for those hanging between living and dying?"

"But there's a need for more at Chetan's, too, right?" Grant asked focusing on Jai.

"True, and there will be, but this is also something that's pressing within society," Jai said, gesturing to the set of documents situated in front of each man at the table. "I gave each of them a set of charts to read and come up with a common denominator."

"What I saw was that every one of the women in those files were obese," Hiram expanded. "The one thing they had in common was they were all raped or molested at early ages. Some of them might have families with generational issues. The mother, the grandmother, even some of the men who were perpetrating the things that had been done to them. That all impacts children on several levels and they carry it into their adult lives."

"You know, you guys are amazing," Grant said accepting another set of documents from Hiram. "And you just sealed the next step that I think you need."

"Somehow that sounds more like a threat, than an attaboy," Kevin said, and a trill of laughter followed.

"Depends on how you look at it," Jai said, scanning the expectant faces in the room. "All of you are going back to school."

The silence that met that statement was thick enough to pour over a stack of blueberry pancakes. One by one, Grant could see confusion, panic, fear and other range of expressions on their faces.

"School?" Hiram croaked.

"Yes. I'm sending your asses back to school, first to get a degree, and then a medical degree of some sort that will give you even more insight between what you've just been able to ascertain from what you've learned by working at Chetan."

"Makes sense," Grant said, holding his fist out for a pound and Jai obliged. "People will give you a lot more weight with everything you put in place with a little educational muscle behind you. And that's not saying that you shouldn't open, it's saying that you should do this in tandem."

"Results are all that matter," Hiram protested, gifting the Knights with a lopsided grin.

"You're right," Grant shot back. "But if you're planning to take this on a national, maybe … international level, you need a little backing before folks try to poke holes in your process."

"International?" Ryan choked out and looked at his fellow Knights. "Whoa."

Jai beamed with pride. "Grant is right. That premise alone will be able to drive you to answers. You'll learn how the medical world views things, then you're able to slice holes in those theories and present your findings worldwide." He shrugged. "Even I hadn't thought to go that route. I was driven by what happened with my grandmother and it has been my guide to Chetan." He briefly broke eye contact to compose himself. "I can't tell you how proud I am that you all will take this even further than I imagined. Now I know how my mentor felt when he encouraged me to think beyond the small world I live in."

"And speaking of thinking beyond one issue to come up with a solution to problems that challenge us," Grant said, realizing that they too, hailed from all areas of Chicago. "Is anyone familiar with

Alderman Knight?"

"Yeah, he's from my neck of the woods," Ryan said, perking up. "What do you need?"

"What can you find out about the things he's doing that might not be … how do I say it?"

"On the up and up," Hiram supplied.

"Yes, what he said." Grant held up both hands. "I don't want any of you going out looking for trouble. I just want to know what you might have heard about him and some of his activities."

Jai shifted forward in his chair. "What's going on, brother?"

Grant folded his hands on the table and said. "Let me fill you in on some things."

CHAPTER 10

Grant left Jai's center, and thanks to the Knights he was armed with a little bit of information that he tucked away for future use. He arrived at the United Center early and was now standing on the hardwood floor where the Chicago Bulls once handled their business. Mostly when Michael Jordan, Dennis Rodman, Scottie Pippen, Bill Wennington, and Luc Longley were in the paint. He was a diehard Houston Rockets fan thanks to his uncle, but the Bulls came in a close second. Grant glanced around the stadium, imagining the architectural changes he proposed and smiled. He couldn't wait to get started.

"Excuse me, may I help you?" A deep voice asked, coming from behind him.

Grant turned to find an armed security guard standing with his right hand resting on a nine-millimeter. The tall, muscular man had a look on his face that screamed he was not to be played with; a sentiment Grant mirrored. Knowing he was only doing his job; Grant adjusted his attitude.

"I'm Grant Khambrel, and I'm here to see Autumn Knight." He felt that familiar ping to his heart just speaking her name. What the hell was wrong with him? It wasn't like he didn't have his pick of women. Why was he feeling anything for a woman with a corrupt father, and more baggage then an airport's carousel. Then Grant thought about Richmond laying claim to Autumn the first time he and Meeks met with James Knight, and his anger amped up. This was more drama than he cared to deal with in his personal life.

Yet, Autumn was a woman who could give Grant a smoldering look from across several feet and would ignite a flame that could burn down any structure in their wake.

"Is Miss. Knight expecting you?"

"Yes, she is," Grant read the man's badge. "Mr. Morgan."

The guard removed a cell from his hip, pushed a couple of numbers, and brought the phone to his ear. "Good morning Jenna, it's Willie and I'm on the floor with a," he pulled the phone from his ear and looked at Grant head-to-toe. "What's your last name again?"

"Khambrel. Grant Khambrel," he replied, trying to keep his annoyance in check.

"He says his name is Grant Khambrel, and he claims to have a meeting with Miss. Knight, but I don't see his name on the register."

Claims. The man was treating him like some vagabond from off the streets instead of a successful business executive wearing a blue Giorgio Armani suit that probably cost more than his monthly salary.

Grant smiled at the excited squeal coming through the phone. He had no idea what the person on the other end of the line had said, but the look on Willie's face was Master Card Priceless.

"Sure thing, I'll take him to the elevator." He ended the call, returned the phone to his hip and pivoted. "This way, Mr. Khambrel."

Grant followed him to the elevator and made the short ride up four flights. When the doors opened, Grant's breath was snatched from his lungs when he was greeted by a stunning woman with the greenest eyes he'd ever seen. Yes, *that* woman.

"Good morning Mr. Khambrel," a sensual voice said, and it was as if everything around him came to a standstill. He literally felt like he was frozen in time. "I'm Autumn Knight. Welcome to the United Center."

Grant's whole being was filled with this spectacular woman's presence. Her magnificent smile spoke to every part of him. The fitted black pantsuit and red scoop neck blouse showcased a perfectly fit body with curves in all the right places. The glimpse of her breast and sweet scent rendered him speechless. Average White Band's *Only A School Boy Crush* came to mind. He almost smiled, but this certainly felt deeper than what was covered in those lyrics.

"Mr. Khambrel," Autumn prompted, offering a delicate hand that was swallowed by Grant's much larger one.

The moment their palms met, a strong current passed between them, and their eyes collided. Grant held her gaze as an intense desire had his blood quickening into every part of his body. "Autumn," he whispered, his body propelled forward as if he was being pulled by a magnet. Grant had never experienced such a reaction to any woman.

Autumn flinched, slowly removed her hand from his and took a step back. Her breathing increase, as evidenced by the rise and fall of her chest. Her beautiful green eyes darkened, and tongue darted from her mouth and wet her lips. *Damn.*

Grant had unwittingly invaded Autumn's personal space. He quickly pulled himself together and put a little more space between them. "It's nice to meet you, and please call me Grant."

"In that case, you can call me Autumn," she replied, drumming her fingers at her side.

"That's a beautiful name." He held her gaze as he tried to control his breathing. "For a beautiful season."

"Thank you." She smiled, lowered her eyes, and pushed a long curly lock of hair behind her ear. Her cheeks reddened, and everything male in Grant responded—against his damn will!

Autumn smiled up at Grant and asked, "How ... how was your trip? You came from Texas, correct?"

Grant could see how his touch affected her and that pleased him immensely. Another first. "Correct, it was fine, thanks for asking."

"All of your supplies and equipment arrived yesterday, and we placed them in the conference room." She gestured toward a long hall that seemed to run the length of the west end of the stadium. "Would you like to get settled in, or would you like to take a quick tour of the area? All the specified locations have been taped off."

Grant needed distance. *Pronto.* Standing next to the woman who had been creeping into his thoughts when he should be focusing on work was wreaking havoc on his system. He needed to get his head back on straight, and the sooner, the better.

"I think it would be best if I get things set up so I can get to work," he said. "There are quite a few plans I need to review and go over before meeting with the construction team."

"About the B&G Construction company, have you met with them yet? Do you know the project leader?" Her tone was sharper than it should have been for such a simple query.

Grant smiled. "I know them very well. We do a lot of work together." He decided to hold back his true connection with the company. Seemed as though she had some issues with B&G, and he intended to find out why and what.

"Oh, well, that should make things easier for all concerned," she said. The disdain was also unexpected. "My assistant, Jenna, is available to assist you if you need anything until you find one of your own."

He gestured for her to take the lead. "Thanks, I would appreciate that, and hopefully it won't take long to find someone."

"No problem. Follow me, and I'll show you to the conference room."

Grant watched Autumn walk away, and it took everything in him not to reach for her. He never yearned for anyone like this before and was determined not to let it control him.

CHAPTER 11

Autumn returned to her office, moved over to the desk, and plopped down in her chair. She reached for the bottled water sitting near the stacks of paperwork she'd been reading and working on when Jenna had advised her of Grant Khambrel's arrival. She cracked the seal and took a very un-ladylike gulp.

Grant Khambrel was the mystery man from the hospital. *How the hell is this happening? He obviously doesn't remember me. That sucks.* She took another drink, wishing it was more of the frozen variety. She needed to cool off because she'd never been affected by a man in such away.

Dating had been nearly impossible under her father's watchful eyes during her teenage years. Her only sexual encounter had been a fumbled experience in the backseat of a car with a football player that had been interrupted by a police officer. Lucky for them, the man was a big football fan. Needless to say, the moment was underwhelming. Her time at Spelman University hadn't fared much better. Somehow every man who even looked her way suddenly gave her the cold shoulder, or seemed to disappear without a trace. It wasn't until she returned home, and she'd caught the attention of Richmond Kane, that she'd given serious thought to the possibility of romance.

Richmond, a Morehouse and Harvard business school graduate, started working for Autumn's father over the summer during his college years. After graduating, Richmond became a full-time associate and somehow set his sights on winning her heart. While Autumn enjoyed spending time with Richmond—he was handsome, successful, being her father's choice for a son-in-law wasn't the qualities she wanted in a mate.

Once again, romance was placed on the back burner. Unfortunately, Richmond was having a hard time processing the fact that she was no longer interested.

While Autumn found Richmond attractive, what she felt for Grant was near other-worldly. The moment their palms met, she was overwhelmed by need and want. For a split second, Autumn forgot to breathe. How the hell did that happen? Even after drinking over half a bottle of water, she still felt hot, especially at the apex of her thighs. Autumn shifted in her seat when there was a knock at her door.

"Come in," she called out, sitting forward.

"Good morning, beautiful," Richmond said as he moseyed into the office, carrying a bouquet of roses. "These are for you."

Lord, I don't like roses. They're either for apologies or first times. Autumn resisted the urge to cross her arms, then came from around the desk. She accepted the flowers and took a whiff before saying, "Thank you, these are beautiful. What's the occasion?"

"You're the occasion," he replied, offering up a megawatt smile. His eyes dropped to Autumn's mouth.

Autumn read his next move and beat him to the punch. She rose up on tiptoes, angled her face away so her kiss landed on the cheek instead of the place he intended. "Thank you, Richmond."

She could swear she heard disappointment in his mumbled words as she moved to place them on the conference table. "I'll get Jenna to put these in water. Now, what's the real reason you're here?"

"I told—"

Autumn raised her right hand, stopping the lie she could almost see forming in his head. "What's the *other* reason you're here Richmond?"

"I thought as long as I was here, I might as well check in on the new architect." He jammed his hands in his pockets. "You know, make sure he's comfortable and has everything he needs."

She placed a hand on her hip. "The last time I checked, I was the Director of Administration and Operations around here. It's *my* job to make sure Mr. Khambrel has *everything* he needs."

Autumn saw the narrowing of Richmond's eyes and knew her words had been taken out of context. Before she could re-phrase herself, Richmond took a step forward and stared down at her.

"You're a very beautiful and desirable woman," he said, his voice took on a familiar edge. "And I would hate for Mr. Khambrel to make any inappropriate moves. Your father and me agree that things between the two of you should remain professional."

Autumn raised her chin defiantly. "I'm a twenty-eight-year-old grown-ass woman. I don't need you or my father trying to direct my personal life as if it's a damn play." She dropped her hands. "With that being said, I'm a professional and have no intention of getting involved with *anyone* affiliated with my father."

Richmond seemed to lose his bravado at that last statement. "I—I didn't mean to upset you or insinuate anything improper," he stammered. "I'm sorry, Autumn."

She gave a nonchalant wave. "Whatever you and my father have cooked up with Mr. Khambrel, I suggest you both leave me the hell out of it."

Richmond rocked on his heels a little bit. "You have to stop being so suspicious of everything we do, Autumn."

How can I when I know better. Autumn sighed, moved out of his reach, and stood behind her desk. "I have a busy day ahead of me. If there's nothing—"

A knock on the door snatched her attention. "Come in."

"Excuse me, Autumn." Jenna stood in the doorway, her eyes cut to Richmond.

"Good morning Mr. Kane," Jenna greeted with a sweet smile that actually reached her eyes.

Richmond gave Jenna an odd look. Autumn wanted to join him. Her assistant was being nice to Richmond. Why?

"Good morning, Jenna," Richmond replied, his voice laced with suspicion.

"What is it Jenna?" Autumn's tone was sharper than she intended.

"Mr. Khambrel would like a moment of your time."

Now she understood. Jenna was trying to impress or at least remain professional in front of Grant.

Richmond folded his arms and leaned against her desk. He had no intention of leaving, which annoyed the hell out of her. "Send him in."

Jenna's forehead creased and gave a quick nod. She escorted Grant in, and the moment he crossed the threshold and their eyes met, Autumn's inner muscles at her core clenched. Her body was reminding her that she was a woman with unfulfilled desires. Lots of them. She could feel Richmond's glare bore into her face.

"Autumn."

"Yes, Grant," she replied.

His gaze shifted, undoubtedly gauging their interaction. "Richmond, I hope I'm not interrupting," he stated, but Autumn could tell from his posture Grant didn't care if he had interrupted anything.

"Actually—"

"We were just finishing up," Autumn said before Richmond could complete his statement. "What can I do for you?"

"I thought I'd take you up on your offer if it's still on the table."

"And exactly what offer might that be?" Richmond asked, frowning.

"*Autumn* so graciously offered to tour me."

She watched as the two men sized each other up. She should stop this nonsense, but she took a moment to do a little sizing herself.

Both men were tall, incredibly handsome, and wore their expensive Italian suits over magnificent bodies like a second skin. Yet, it was Grant who had her body responding in ways she didn't understand. He invoked desire she'd only read about in romance novels and could only dream of experiencing.

Richmond tilted his head. "Did she now?"

Autumn knew Richmond was annoyed by the way Grant said her name. The way he said it wrapped around her like a warm welcome blanket.

"Well, as she was just pontificating about how busy she was, how about I do the honors?" Richmond offered.

Pontificating? Oh, college boy is out for blood. Autumn narrowed her eyes and glared at Richmond. "I'm sure you're quite busy yourself. Doesn't my father have some *errand* you need to run for him?" She knew she'd hit the bullseye when Richmond dropped his hands and straightened his stance.

"As a matter fact he does. And since we both know how much you dislike our business discussions in your presence, this is more reason for me to tour your guest. We have unfinished business. Shall we, Grant." He gestured towards the door.

Grant kept his gaze on Autumn for several moments, causing Richmond to stew.

She conceded with a smile and Grant said, "Sure." He continued to keep his attention on Autumn. "I'm not certain about what he's implying here, but I'll check back with you later to answer any questions you might have."

"That won't be—"

Autumn cut a look at Richmond that made him clamp down on whatever he had to say.

She nodded to Grant and watched the two men leave the office together. Grant glanced over his shoulder giving her a lingering look while ignoring Richmond's impatience.

Part of her was curious as to what type of business Grant could possibly have with Richmond and her father. Whatever it was, wasn't hers and she needed to stay clear of both men.

Too bad her treacherous body wasn't getting the message.

CHAPTER 12

"I'm sure you can understand, Mr. Knight only wants what's best for his only daughter… his only child," Richmond stated as they made their way around the first level of the stadium. "I mean, you're an only child. Your uncle raised you, right?"

"I am, and he did," Grant reluctantly confirmed, trying to keep his annoyance in check.

"I'm sure, like Mr. Knight, your uncle did everything he could to make sure you had a good life." He stopped walking. "He made sure nothing or no one got in the way of all the plans he had for you."

Grant fixed his eyes on Richmond. "No, he didn't, but he also made sure I was prepared to make my own decisions." *This ass doesn't give a damn about the alderman's plans for Autumn, he's worried about his own.*

Richmond never outright said for Grant to keep his hands to himself, but he got the message. What the man didn't know was that he had every intention of doing just that. The last thing Grant needed was to have his nose so far wide open behind Autumn that he'd be standing in the middle of the street in broad daylight searching for her with a flashlight.

Enough already. Grant widened his stance and placed his back against the nearest wall. "Why don't we get to the real reason you're here?"

Richmond exhaled noisily. "Fine." He matched Grant's posture while keeping his hands at his sides. "The alderman and I have a press conference tomorrow morning, and we need to prepare our agenda. Do we announce your disqualification, or offer our official and sincere congratulations?"

Grant wanted to knock that smug look right off Richmond's face. Unfortunately, without any additional information he had to play along. "What type of access are you wanting, specifically?"

"We understand there are quite a few changes coming to the Castle, and we want to be sure that local vendors are used for key services."

So, they were back to playing that game. "Khalil has always used local vendors to provide services to the Castle."

"Yes, but we have a vendors' list we want you to publicly endorse, and of course, use." Richmond pulled out his phone and hit several keys. "I just emailed you the list."

"And what exactly do you get out of the deal?"

"Just doing our civic duty."

Like hell. Grant's phone chimed. He pulled out his cell, angled it so Richmond couldn't see as he read the text. "Looks like you and the alderman want a monopoly on services."

"It's all for the good of the community," he claimed, shrugging.

"There are several local vendors already being considered and vetted. You do know I'm not the only King of that Castle," Grant stated.

"Yeah, we know, it's what, eight or nine of you now?" Richmond countered. "You all swooped in and took control without considering the people you would be ousting. Or how all of your changes would affect those who had already invested time, money and energy in that Castle," he said with disgust in his voice that he didn't try to hide. "We also know how much power you wield and how persuasive you can be."

How and where is this man getting his information?

"We expect full compliance with our request." Grant's eyebrow shot up and Richmond quickly amended, "at least the majority of the request. Any vendor you can't get placed at the Castle put them here. Just put our vendors to work."

Grant had to buy time. Final contract awards for all vendors wouldn't be issued for another ten months. "I'll talk to the other Kings."

"Talk all you want," Richmond said with another infuriating smirk. "Just make it happen."

A vein throbbed at Grant's temple. He held Richmond's gaze and gave a quick nod.

"Good man, Mr. Knight will be pleased to hear it. Tomorrow's press conference will go off without a hitch." He took a step forward and slid both hands in his pockets. "On another note, keep things professional with Autumn. She's not meant for someone like you."

Grant smirked. "Have a good day Richmond," he said before walking in the direction that would take him back to Autumn's office.

His phone vibrated. He checked the screen, and it read restricted. "Grant Khambrel."

"I need you to add one more name to that list Richmond just gave you."

"Who is this?" Grant paused his movements, glanced over his

shoulders to find Richmond making his way around the corner.

"That's irrelevant. Liberty Consulting, add them as well." Grant could tell the caller's voice was being altered. "What type of consulting—"

"Not your concern," he snapped. "Just do as I say or—"

"You'll have my contract pulled. I know." Grant couldn't hide his sarcasm.

The caller laughed. "I don't give a damn about your contract. I'll leave that for Alderman Knight. What I do care about is justice and restitution."

"What—"

"Just do as you're told, and everyone will get what they deserve." The line dropped.

Grant heard the anger in the caller's voice, and it reviled his own. Something more was going on, and he knew what had to be done. This was happening on Chicago turf. Grant called the one man he knew could help with this very specific need.

"Daron, it's Grant. Hit me up when you get this message."

As a successful security specialist that developed and produced specialized security systems, Daron had managed to take down Chase Preston's family business from the inside. Bringing down an international crime ring could have had deadly repercussions, but somehow Daron had been able to keep his direct involvement under wraps.

Grant walked into the conference room, removed his jacket, draping it across the chair before taking a seat at the table. He pulled out his phone and placed a call. "Meeks, you got a second?"

"Yeah, what's up?"

"Richmond paid me a visit at the center. They wanted an answer immediately." He heard Meeks frustrated sigh before releasing a string of profanity. "I couldn't stall."

After calming down, Meeks said, "Well, since I haven't heard anything on the news about a multimillion-dollar renovation contract for the United Center being pulled, I can only assume you caved into the Alderman's demands. What did you agree to do?

"Daddy, junior and Frankie won't play tea party no more. Fix it!" Grant heard Meeks three-year-old daughter say in a demanding tone. She sounded so cute Grant couldn't help but smile. While Meeks' daughter may be a beautiful carbon copy of her mother with long curly hair and green eyes, apparently, she inherited her father's sunny disposition. "Like father, like daughter."

"You have no idea."

"I bet," Grant replied, chuckling.

"Give me a minute."

"Sure," Grant replied, anxious to hear the outcome of this epic battle.

"Sweetheart, daddy is on the phone can you go tell mommy?"

"No, daddy, mommy told me to tell you to handle it. 'Member, mommy got three new babies in her belly to take care of right now. I want sisters," she demanded.

Grant threw his head back and laughed so hard he lost his balance and almost fell out of his chair. At least the little minx was getting some of what she wanted. Meeks had told Grant already they were having two girls and a boy. With six children, his friend was going to have his hands full, and Grant knew Meeks wouldn't have it any other way.

"Okay," was the jubilant reply before a stern, "let me finish my call, and I'll have tea with you."

"Yay! Now hurry up, daddy."

Grant felt a warm sensation pass through his body with thoughts of Autumn. The pain Grant experienced losing his parents at such a young age had him burying any desire to have a wife and children. He couldn't imagine leaving his family to experience the things he had, no matter how great things eventually turned out. For some reason, the idea of having a little girl who looked like Autumn didn't scare him at all. *Where the hell did that come from?*

"Grant … Grant you still there?"

"Yeah, I'm here."

"Sorry about that, daddy duty. We have about ten minutes before we're interrupted again and she says the tea's getting cold," he explained. "What did you agree to?"

"They want me to use their list of preferred vendors at the Castle."

"Preferred vendors, huh?" Meeks scoffed. "I guess Mark was right."

"And they're all related service companies." Grant rolled his neck trying to release the tension. "But here's the kicker. After Raymond left, I received another mystery call with some additional instructions and claiming to have evidence." After explaining the new demand, he said, "I have no idea what this proof they claim to have could be, but there's obviously more to this threat then we realized."

"So, it seems," Meeks mused, and Grant could "hear" the thoughts rolling through his friend's mind. "At least this buys us time to try and turn the tables on the good alderman. If we can find proof that he altered the proposal or evidence of his dirty dealings, we're in the clear."

"As well as finding out who else is blackmailing me, if it's not him," Grant reminded his friend.

"True."

"What about Mark?" Grant reached for the stress ball that sat on his desk, a gift from his uncle. "Did you find out anything?"

"He's clean. I'll send you the report after my tea party."

Grant smirked. "You do that, but one more thing."

"What?"

"I'm bringing Daron Kincaid up to speed on the rest of what's going on. After all, he's the king in charge of the security for the Castle as well as all the Kings."

"Why not bring in Alejandro," Meeks countered. "He's your fixer, right?"

Alejandro Reyes, Dro, as he preferred to be called, was a professional problem solver and had been one his entire life. His company, Vantage Point, focused on crisis management and repairing professional reputations. Dro's company was booming and in high demand in the Windy City.

Grant loosened his shirt and rubbed the back of his neck. "True, but…"

"But what?" Meeks prompted.

"Dro is the perfect person to fix any problems that may surface as a result of all our digging or what we might find. In fact, I'm pretty sure he'll need to pull out his industrial scrub brush for all the dirt we may turn up."

"Good point and Dro's the best in the business."

"And no offense to you, Dro, or Jed for that manner, but Daron still has contacts and access to places and people in Chicago that I have a feeling might know the types of people who'd be blackmailing me." He tossed the stress ball to his other hand. "After all, they're coming after me for something my uncle did years ago." Grant released a humorless laugh. "You know, before becoming my guardian Uncle Ben lived an adventurous and sometimes unsavory lifestyle with men who made their living crossing several lines. Ben's words, not mine."

Meeks remained silent a moment, then said, "I get that, but you'd be surprised how low we can go if necessary. We'll focus on the alderman, and whatever's going on at the hotel."

"And I'll see if Daron can help with that other thing."

"Daddy," Grant heard the little one yell in the background.

"Coming sweet girl. Duty calls. Talk later." Meeks ended the call.

Grant stood and stretched. He checked his watch, a Piaget Emperador Cushion which was a gift from his uncle after they signed their first multi-million-dollar government contract. Realizing he must be finished with his daily swim; Grant dialed his uncle.

"Hello, son."

"Uncle Ben, how are you?"

"I'm doing all right."

"How was your swim?"

"It was fine. How are you? I expected to have heard from you before now."

Grant could hear the disappointment in his voice.

Uncle Ben would prefer to talk to him every day, but he understood Grant was a busy man, so their scheduled Monday, Wednesday, and Friday calls were acceptable. His uncle figured a hard-working man needed to spend his weekends recharging his battery and relaxing doing other things, and not talking to his kinfolk. However, things had been so crazy that Grant had missed their Monday call. He had sent a text, but Uncle Ben liked hearing his voice. Rightfully so.

"I apologize. Things have been much busier than I expected."

"I'm sure you can handle it."

Grant leaned against the desk. "I'm trying. How's Sam?"

Uncle Ben had always been openly gay, but when ten-year-old Grant came to live with him, he had kept that part of his life private and away from his orphaned nephew. He ended a long-term relationship so he could focus all his attention where he felt it should be placed. Thankfully, once Grant left for Atlanta, Georgia to attend Morehouse College, Ben opened himself up for love again when he met Samuel Pack, a fellow chef.

"He's fine. Making a nuisance of himself," he said, laughing.

Grant shook his head. He knew that meant Sam was making sure his uncle took care of himself, and for that he was grateful. Sam was more than a little skeptical about Grant asking Ben to send his medical records to Jai for him to come up with an alternative health plan. The chemo didn't seem to be working as well, and it seemed like his uncle was wasting away. His king brother had called on Felicia Blake, Meeks' sister-in-law, in an effort to come up with a treatment that may save his uncle's life.

"Well, tell him I said hello and keep up the good work." His phone beeped. He looked at the screen and sighed with relief. "Uncle Ben, I have to take this. I'll call you later."

"Be sure you do."

Grant clicked over. "Daron."

"What's up?"

"I need help from the King of Morgan Park."

CHAPTER 13

Autumn completed what had to be the most boring conference call ever. It didn't help that her wayward thoughts kept landing on the good-looking man working down the hall. She glanced over at the sack lunch Jenna provided. Autumn was diligently working through the lunch hour, and the idea of eating a simple sandwich suddenly lost its appeal. She reached for the bag, resigned her stomach to its fate, when a knock at the door made her pause mid-reach.

"Come in," she called out.

The door swung open, and Grant leaned into the doorway. His shirt sleeves were rolled up, and his arms folded across his chest. "I see you have lunch already. I was hoping I could convince you to join me."

Autumn's pulse quickened as she stared into the face of her walking wet dream. She could feel her cheeks warm for even thinking of such a thing. Autumn tried to keep her heart from pounding erratically as she reached inside the bag and pulled out a tuna fish sandwich that could go swim in Lake Michigan for all she cared. She held it up and asked, "You have something better than this?"

Grant dropped his arms, pushed off the door, walked up to her desk and offered his hand. "As a matter fact, I do."

She stared up at him before dropping her eyes to his hand. Autumn dropped the sandwich back in the bag, slowly came to her feet and placed her hand in his. As expected, the warmth of his body flowed through hers and their gazes collided.

"Come, everything's set up in the conference room."

Autumn came from around the desk and grabbed her cell. "Please leave it. Jenna knows where you'll be if something important comes up. I've already turned mine off. I want one hour of uninterrupted time with you. Grant flashed an ear to ear smile and intertwined their fingers. "Shall we?"

Grant led Autumn out the door and past a grinning Jenna, who tried to pretend she was reading the document she held—a document that was upside down. Autumn paused, inched backward, plucked the paper from Jenna's hand and turned it right side up. Then stepped back to Grant and proceeded down the hall.

Jenna released a hardy laugh.

They entered the conference room that had been converted to his office, and Autumn stopped in her tracks. She pulled her hand free and stood in awe of what lay in her wake.

To accommodate his adjustable drawing table, steel assembly table, and multipurpose desk, the large conference table and chairs had been removed. Yet in the middle of what she could only assume was an architect's dream setup, a beautiful table for two had been laid out. A linen tablecloth, crystal stemware, flowers, and two plates with silver covers decorated the table.

"Why ... how did you do all this?"

Grant stood with his hands by his sides. His eyes roamed her body head to toe, and she wondered if her scoop neck blouse was showing more than she realized. Autumn wanted to check, but when his eyes found hers, she held firm.

"You are outstandingly beautiful, and from the moment I saw you I haven't been able to get you off my mind." His mouth twisted into something that looked like the cat that ate the canary. "I hope you don't find that too creepy."

Maybe he does remember me after all?

"Little bit," she mocked, giving him a lopsided grin. "After all, we just officially met a few hours ago."

Grant walked over to the table and pulled out the chair. "Please, sit, eat with me, and I'll explain. Hopefully, you'll find me a lot less creepy."

Autumn claimed the seat he offered. "I hope you like strawberry lemonade," Grant asked, reaching for a silver container.

"I do. I'm surprised you do."

"Why, because I'm a man," he asked, tipping the sweet pink liquid into their ice-filled glasses.

"Pretty much, I guess that's a little sexist of me," she admitted, laughing, then took a sip from her glass. Autumn was nervous and had to pull herself together. "This is good."

Grant steeled into the seat across from Autumn, gesturing towards the covered plates. "Shall we see what's for lunch?"

"Not until you explain why I shouldn't find this to be creepy."

Grant sat back in the chair and released an audible sigh. "Today wasn't the first time I saw you."

He did remember. Autumn's brows snapped together. "When—"

"Let me explain." Grant held up both hands as if to yield. "Do you know who Khalil Germaine is?"

"Yes, of course," she replied. "Everyone in Chicago knows him, if not the world. The man is damn near a saint in some people's eyes. Except father, because he can't get to him like he has with so many other powerful people."

He lowered his hands. "Well, he was my teacher, my mentor. If it wasn't for him and my uncle Ben, who raised me after my parents died when I was just a boy, I'm not sure where I'd be."

"Oh, Grant, I'm sorry." She reached out and squeezed his wrist. Her need to comfort him was overwhelming, and she didn't understand why. Maybe the loss of her mother had something to do with it.

He placed his hand over hers, and Autumn's throat went dry. She pulled back her hand and reached for her glass. After taking another drink, she asked, "When was the first time you saw me?"

"You were visiting someone at Northwestern Medical Hospital when I was there visiting Khalil. I was standing at the nurses' station waiting on word of how he was doing when I looked up into the greenest eyes I'd ever seen. You smiled at me, and I knew I had to meet you. I took a couple steps towards you when the nurse called me back. Before I turned to leave, I looked over my shoulder, and you were being escorted out by a man who I now know was your father."

Autumn bit her bottom lip, a flush crept up her face and she shivered. "So that brief encounter prompted all this?"

"Pretty much," he nodded. "Still creepy?"

Seeing the sincerity in his eyes, Autumn reached for the lid. "Let's see what's for lunch." A slow smile spread across her face. "You ordered from Lou Malnati's, or should I say Jenna did?"

"She's an excellent assistant," Grant stated, grinning while removing his lid. "Shall we enjoy lunch while it's hot?"

The pizza's not the only thing that's hot. "Of course."

* * *

Grant exhaled. The thought of Autumn leaving and not allowing them to spend this time together had nearly killed his appetite, not to mention sending him into pre-mature heart failure. His insides began to stir as Autumn bite into Big Lou—a thick crust pizza with everything. She closed her eyes and released a soft moan. A sound that went straight to his groin and one he wanted to hear again, only under more intimate circumstances. Grant was thankful he was still sitting down. Autumn might find his physical response to her moans more than a little creepy.

"How's the pizza?" a husky tone escaped his throat.

Autumn opened her eyes and blushed. She picked up a cloth napkin and wiped her mouth. "It's delicious. Malnati's is one of my favorite restaurants."

"You don't say," he replied, taking a bit of his pie.

They spent the next several minutes making small talk and discussing the recent trades the Bulls had made during the offseason. Grant enjoyed being able to discuss the intricacies of the game with any knowledgeable basketball fan, but a gorgeous woman who ignited his desires was almost too good to be true. Not only could Autumn keep up, she pushed back when she deemed it necessary.

Damn, where have you been all my life?

She gave Grant a scrutinizing gaze as she took a swallow from her glass. "Who are you, Grant Khambrel?"

He reached for the napkin, wiped his mouth, and tossed it on the table. "What would you like to know?"

"Everything."

Grant checked his watch. "We don't have enough time for *everything*. However, if you allow me to take you to dinner tonight, we can give it a start."

Autumn laughed and the sound echoed off the walls sending tremors throughout his body. "Smooth, Mr. Khambrel, very smooth. We barely finished lunch, and you're offering to feed me again."

"Whatever it takes because I'd really like to get to know you, Ms. Knight."

Her whole face lit up, and it made Grant feel desire so intense that he wanted to act reckless and take Autumn hard and fast against the nearest wall—damn the consequence which was an exciting new experience for him. Grant never needed anything or anyone. Until now. He stood and helped Autumn out of her chair, took both of her hands in his and gazed into her eyes. Grant slowly lowered his head, gauging for any resistance as Autumn raised up on tiptoes to meet his kiss. He had every intention of making this first kiss short and sweet.

Once Autumn parted her lips, allowing Grant complete access, something snapped, and the kiss grew passionate quickly. They devoured each other as if their very existence depended on the ability to savor their tastes. The necessity to breathe made Grant break off the kiss, but his lips remained on Autumn's skin. His need to smell and taste it before returning to her mouth was overwhelming—the desire to mate with his woman was powerful.

His woman, from that first look.

Autumn moved her arms up and around Grant's neck, making it clear that she didn't want to stop what they were doing either. Grant's hands explored her body, slowly making their way under her blouse. He groaned in Autumn's mouth when his hands came in contact with her soft skin. Making quick work of unhooking the bra's front clasp, freeing her ample breast, Grant released her tongue and lowered his head. His lips and teeth grazed her nipples before taking them into his mouth. Grant sucked, pulled, and marked Autumn eliciting sounds of satisfaction that had him hard and throbbing.

Grant reluctantly released her breast and tightened his hold. He wanted Autumn to feel how much she was affecting him as he ravaged her mouth. He knew she received the message when she swiveled her hips against his groin and moaned in his mouth. His hand made its way into her pants, under her panties and over the smooth skin to her womanly core where he inserted first one then another finger.

"Damn, baby, you're wet and tight." He ran his tongue across her lips.

"Oh, yes," she whispered.

"Open your eyes, sweetheart. I want to watch you come." He increased his strokes, witnessed her haggard breathing and saw the moment her climax hit. Grant brought his mouth down on hers to capture the sound of her release.

He kissed Autumn until her shivers eased, and she relaxed in his arms. Grant brought his fingers to his mouth. "Sweet…"

"Oh, wow," she whispered.

Grant leaned his forehead against hers. "What time do I pick you up tonight?"

"You don't."

Grant raised his head and confusion hit him like a bolt of lightning. "I don't?"

Autumn tightened her hold. "No, but you can arrive at my place at seven. We'll have a lot more privacy, and I'll cook."

He raised an eyebrow. "You can cook?"

She gave him a playful nudge.

Grant smiled and lowered his head, but the sound of someone aggressively knocking stopped him short of his goal.

Autumn stepped out of his hold and fully adjusted her clothes before saying, "Come in."

The door opened, and a grinning Jenna walked in, holding a pink note. "Sorry to intrude, but I have a message for you, and he said it was urgent."

Autumn took a step forward.

"No, it's for Grant."

Grant accepted the note as he thanked Jenna for all of her help. The call was from Meeks, and it was marked urgent with multiple exclamation points. He grabbed the cell from his desk and said, "I apologize, but I have to take this."

CHAPTER 14

Autumn returned to her office and paced as if she was on a walking track determined to get those final daily steps in.

She couldn't believe her wanton display with Grant—a man she barely knew. But when he kissed her, touched her, Autumn's body went up in flames, and she had lost every ounce of control. Autumn had even invited Grant over to her house for dinner, for goodness sakes. She leaned against the edge of her desk and dropped her head in her hands.

"Wow, that must have been some lunch. I have to get by Malnati's more often." She leaned her head slightly to the left. "Or was it the man that's got you in such a frenzy?"

Autumn stood, nervously fiddled with her blouse, rounded her desk, and slid into the executive chair. "Close the door and get over here."

Jenna complied. "What's up?" She asked, taking a seat across from the desk from Autumn.

"Why did you help Grant set all that up?"

"Seriously? When a sexy, single, wealthy and kind-hearted man, did I say he was single, sexy and kind-hearted? When a man like that asks you to help him plan a nice lunch for a woman he likes—"

"He told you that he likes me?" Autumn sat forward, and the corners of her mouth turned up. Almost like she was back in high school, giggling about boys.

Jenna laughed. "He didn't have to. His instructions were very specific. Not to mention ..."

"Not to mention what?"

"Girl, his face was lit-up like one big Christmas bulb the more he talked about what he wanted me to do. He said he wanted to make lunch special for you. To keep it simple but make it your favorites."

"Really?"

"Duh, and by the look on your face, it must have been some lunch." Jenna waved her hand in front of Autumn. "Plus, you forgot to re-tuck your shirt in the back."

She gave her friend the evil eye while fixing her attire before saying, "That doesn't matter. The office is not the place for such behavior."

Jenna wiggled her eyebrows. "What type of behavior?"

"Never mind." Autumn turned towards her computer. "I have tons of work to deal with, and so do you."

"Okay, be that way." Jenna rose and headed for the door.

"Jenna?"

"Yeah," she stopped and looked over her shoulders.

"Thank you."

"Anytime. You have two hours before your meeting with York Adams," she reminded her before closing the door.

She leaned back in her chair. "And I was having such a great day."

York Adams, a Ward superintendent, was one of her father's minions. Before her father set his sights on Richmond as his heir apparent, he tried to push Autumn to date York. The man was handsome enough, but he wanted to ascend to her father's throne a bit too much for her taste. The man even assumed Autumn would sleep with him the first time she'd agreed to allow him to escort her to a charity event. That wasn't her style. At least it hadn't been until about an hour or ago.

She could still taste Grant on her tongue. Sweet Lord!

Until today, in this town, Autumn didn't think there were any good independent men left. Men who didn't try to emulate someone else, men who thought for themselves, and were driven by their ambitions. Autumn licked her lips, felt how much they were marked by his efforts. She reached for her phone and texted her housekeeper. Autumn needed a few things from the store. She had a guest coming for dinner, and she couldn't wait.

* * *

Grant walked down to an unoccupied area and dialed Meeks.

"It's about time." He could hear the annoyance in his friend's voice. "Why was your phone off? Francine was about five minutes away from having Jed ascend on the United Center to find you."

"My phone wasn't off. It was on silent. You obviously still have the ability to track me down," Grant reminded Meeks feeling like a child being chastised by worried parents.

"Doesn't matter."

"Why—"

"That sixth sense thing Francine has with her sisters seems to have extended to others now. People close to her, folks she considers family. She felt you were experiencing deep emotions, or something was going on with you, but she couldn't tell if it was good or bad."

Meeks' wife, part of a trio of sisters who were near-identical triplets except for their eye color, was known to have silent conversations with her sisters and have "feelings" about things. It had been something that Grant had witnessed but hadn't completely bought into until now. He had definitely been experiencing something—desire of the most intense type.

"No, I mean, why the urgency in reaching me?"

"We traced a couple of fat foreign bank accounts in James Knight's name. It looks like we might have found where his blackmail proceeds are going."

"How can you be sure? It could very well be legit money he's trying to hide from the IRS," Grant speculated, wondering why he was trying to give the dirty aldermen the benefit of the doubt.

You know why. You have a thing for his daughter.

"We won't know anything for sure until we find one of the victims. Then we'll trace the money and have our very own leverage against the man himself."

"That's good news, but it doesn't warrant the urgency displayed."

"There's more."

"Let's have it," Grant pushed, bracing for answers he wasn't sure he wanted.

He heard Meeks shift his phone from one ear to the other. Grant knew that meant he wasn't alone but needed privacy. "There was a second signer on the account, Autumn Knight."

Grant's heart sank. He closed his eyes to take that information in. His gut was telling him there was no way in hell the woman he'd just spent time with, tasted, touched, and wanted more than anything else, could be involved with any of this mess. "That doesn't mean a thing. Her father could've added her to the account without her knowledge."

"Possibly, but we found a completed signature card on file."

"I don't give a damn what you found, Meeks." Grant took a deep breath and exhaled it slowly.

Meeks held his tongue, and Grant knew why. He was giving his friend time to process this new information more rationally.

"How did you find out about all of this so fast?"

"Robert's handling the electronic investigation," Meeks explained.

"I thought he was on another gig."

"He was, but after we found that signature card, Francine had one of her *feelings* and pulled him so he could focus on resolving this case for you. She felt it was important to you."

Francine was right, and Grant knew if anyone could find the truth by following someone's electronic trail, Robert was that guy. "Good, but I don't want anyone jumping to any conclusions about Autumn."

"We won't, but neither should you," Meeks warned. "Based on your response, the level of urgency seems appropriate."

Grant released a deep sigh. "From the moment I saw her, I knew. I've never felt that way about any woman before ... ever," he emphasized, his voice lowered. "It's more than just a physical attraction."

"I completely understand, trust me. Francine says our love is what romance novels and movies are made of."

Both men laughed and said, "Women."

Grant headed back to his office, "I don't know about all that."

"But what I can tell you is that my love for Francine and our children is what keeps me alive," he admitted barely above a whisper.

"I get that, but I don't have a name for what I'm feeling," Grant admitted. "Not yet, at least. What I do know is that I don't believe Autumn is involved, man."

"Well, if she's not, we'll find that out, too. We're combing through the bank's electronic surveillance systems to see if anything pops. Everything's not online, so Robert may have to take a trip." Grant inhaled, but then Meeks continued. "Don't ask. We may have to get creative with looking for the information we need, and that can take some time. In the meantime, be careful, please."

"Will do, thanks." Grant ended the call and dialed Daron.

A hushed tone answered, "Yes, Grant."

"You asleep?" Grant checked the time. "It's the middle of the afternoon."

"Some of us work all hours of the day and night Grant and try to snatch some shut eye when we can."

A moan echoed on the other end. "Sounds like more than a nap."

"What do you want now Grant?"

"An update."

"You just put me on the case a few hours ago," Daron reminded Grant, his frustration coming through loud and clear. *Well, if I'd been disturbed in the middle of an afternoon delight, I'd be pissed too.*

Grant had given Daron the full breakdown on everything going on as well as his suspicions about the Alderman. He was hesitant to ask for Daron's help because of the danger it could pose to his King brother. Daron assured Grant that he could move through the shadows whenever necessary and that he would be fine.

"The people I need to talk to don't work regular nine-to-five jobs. When I find out something, you'll be the first to know." Daron released a low groan. "Hey, cut that out."

Recognizing the sound, Grant knew it was time to end the call, but he didn't get the chance.

"Hi, Grant. Bye, Grant," he heard the soft sweet voice of Daron's great love, whisper. The words were so clear she had to be in his face, which meant he'd been spot on.

"Bye, Cameron," Grant replied just before the call dropped.

For the first time in Grant's life, he envied something someone else had. He wanted that same closeness with Autumn, but he had to clear her name and untangle Autumn from her father's illegal activities before he took their relationship to the next level.

And they would be taking things to the next level. Whether she knew it or not.

CHAPTER 15

Autumn stood next to her desk as she waited for Jenna to escort York into the office. She had every intention of making this meeting quick. Getting home and preparing dinner for Grant suddenly became her number one priority. She planned to dazzle Grant with her culinary skills and delicious cuisine. They said the way to a man's heart was through his stomach. Autumn planned to please his belly as well as other parts of his anatomy in hopes of capturing that elusive muscle in his chest. The door opened, and Autumn plastered on a fake smile.

"Good afternoon, beautiful lady," York said as he entered the office. He stopped in front of Autumn and pulled her into his arms.

"Good afternoon." She quickly stepped out of his hold and walked behind her desk. He had a tendency to be a bit touchy for her liking. "What can I do for you?"

Disappointment flashed in his expression, "Can we sit?"

No. "Sure." Autumn took a seat, intertwined her fingers, and placed them on her desk. "What's going on?"

"I came by to talk a little business with the owner of the construction company that won the renovation bid." He sat forward and rested his forearms against her desk. "But before I did, I thought we could have a chat."

My father sent you here to make sure your side deal is in place. We have nothing to chat about, so get the hell out of my office.

"No one from the construction company has arrived yet," she offered, hoping to move the conversation forward and him towards the door.

"Not according to your father. He said Richmond met with him here this morning," he stated with a puzzled expression.

Autumn nodded, figuring out the problem. "Oh, that explains the confusion. Richmond had a meeting with the architect."

"Yes, Grant Khambrel. He owns a construction company too." His frown deepened as he peered at her.

Autumn's hands fell open, and she sat forward. "What?"

"B&G Construction, it's his company." His brows drew together. "You didn't know? I understand the B stands for Benjamin, his uncle's same, and of course, the G stands for Grant."

"I had no idea," she murmured, and a wave of pain slammed into her belly. "He's the architect, and his construction company was selected to make the renovations?"

York grinned and rubbed his hands together like an evil villain. "Yep, your father's quite pleased, too. He thinks very highly of the guy."

"I'm sure he does." Autumn fought back against the wave of sadness that was threatening her ability to focus. She thought just maybe she'd found a guy worthy of pursuing. Instead she's been duped by another one of the men slated to become her father's minion.

"I stopped by to see if you had plans for dinner." He held up his right hand. "Before you answer, I'd like for you to consider giving us a real chance. The few dates we had—"

"They weren't dates, York." She shot back. "You escorted me to a few charity events at my father's request."

The corner of York's mouth quirked up. "It wasn't a hardship. You're a very beautiful woman."

"Thank you."

"We had fun, didn't we?" His smile widened.

"I've got a lot going on right now, and dating is far down the list." *Especially now.*

"Maybe I should help you make it a higher priority."

Autumn's desk phone rang. "Excuse me." She raised the phone to her ear and said, "Yes, Jenna."

"Grant's here to see you." A warm shiver ran down her spine, and she wanted to kick herself. She couldn't let herself fall for him, especially now.

"Send him in," she replied, disconnecting as she murmured, "Speak of the devil."

The door opened, and Grant walked in, the smile he offered didn't quite reach his eyes. Something was wrong. Concern was growing inside of her, but she quickly tamped it down. Whatever was bothering him was not her problem. Too bad her heart hadn't received the memo.

"Grant, good timing. I want to introduce you to York Adams. He's our ward superintendent." She turned her attention to York. "And I'd like you to meet the United Center winning architect and owner of B&G Construction, it seems."

She saw Grant's jaw clench, and his expression dulled.

Yes, I know the truth. Why didn't you tell me?

Autumn folded her hands and dropped them on her lap as she watched the two men shake hands and exchange pleasantries.

"I was hoping to talk a little business with you if you have a moment. The alderman suggested I stop by," York explained.

* * *

Grant cut his eyes to Autumn. She knew the truth and wasn't happy. Autumn's demeanor towards him had evidently changed, and she was all business, cool and professional. Did her father send this man here to reinstate his demands? And was Autumn making sure they connected? Was that her role in their game?

"Sure, but I need a moment with Autumn," Grant explained to York feeling the weight of Autumn's angry stare.

"Of course—"

"Actually, that won't be necessary." She waved him off. "My father sent York here to discuss business with you. Then it must be important. Right?" Her eyes darted between both men.

"Really?" Grant's eyes bounced between York and Autumn. "Well, if it's that important, I guess you have to excuse us."

Autumn folded her arms in put them in her lap. Both men headed for the door. "York, I'm set up in the conference room down the hall, can you meet me there? I need that minute with Autumn, after all."

"Sure." York looked over at Autumn, his tone resolute as he said, "Think about what we discussed."

The look exchanged between York and Autumn gave Grant an idea of what he wanted her to think about, and he didn't like it one bit. Feeling possessive of anyone was another new sensation that wasn't comfortable for him.

Grant watched the other man, who was observably interested in his woman, walk out and move past Jenna's desk. He closed the door, turned and peered at Autumn.

She sat back in the chair; her face expressionless. "What do you want Grant?"

You, dammit.

He placed both hands in his pockets before he did something foolish like pull her out of her chair, kiss her until she was weak while working his hands under her blouse again. He wanted to touch her, taste her, bury himself so deep inside Autumn she would think somehow she'd grown a new appendage.

"Grant, I asked you a question," she repeated.

Her question brought him back to the conversation. "Something came up. I'm going to have to postpone dinner."

Autumn shrugged. "Fine. In fact, why don't we cancel it altogether? Keep things professional."

His eyebrows snapped together. "Why would we do that, there's unmistakably something going on between us."

"Something that doesn't need to go any further," she said in a matter-of-fact tone that sounded firm and final.

Grant stared into her beautiful green eyes, and his heart raced. He knew she was angry because he had not been upfront about his construction company. She was entitled to an explanation, but first, Grant had to find a way to clear Autumn's name. Then he could convince her that their being together was inevitable, but for now, he would concede to her request.

"If that's what you want."

They continued to stare in silence. Separated by mere steps, the passion flowing between the two of them was palpable. There had to be an explanation for the information Robert found. No way would

Autumn have anything to do with her father's unethical and illegal behavior. For years, he'd been a good judge of character. It had only failed in one regard and that had been while in his twenties.

"By the way, my director of construction operations, AJ Cook, will arrive with the first wave of the construction crew tomorrow."

"Fine, I'll look forward to meeting him." Autumn picked up a file and opened it as if dismissing him.

He could only hope that what Meeks and Daron turned up would clear her completely.

CHAPTER 16

"Knock…knock," Jenna asked as she entered Autumn's office. "Ready to go? Because I certainly am."

"It's Friday and girls' night out." She hit the off button on her computer, pulled her purse out her desk drawer, and stood. "You're always ready. Let me change my shoes."

"Please do, I'd hate to show you up in my new Jimmy Choo's." She took several steps back and stuck out her right foot and rotated it.

Autumn nodded. "Nice." The glitter pointed-toe pump went nicely with the short black sequenced dress she'd changed in to. "Why are you so dressed up? We're just going to happy hour at the Ogden bar down the street, or did I miss something?"

"No, but a few of us are going clubbing after happy hour. I'd invite you, but we both know how much you like clubbing," Jenna said, sarcasm lacing her tone.

She slipped her feet into the black Coco Chanel shoes which sat under her desk. She thought they were perfect to be paired with the pink and black Chanel mini dress. "I might surprise you one day and join you."

Jenna's face brightened with excitement. "Then—"

"But not today." She laughed, coming around her desk. "Let's go, we don't want to keep the girls waiting."

As they made their way out the office and down the hall, Autumn couldn't help but wonder what Grant was up to tonight. It was Friday night, and he was back in Texas. It had been a week since Grant left town to handle a few business matters back home. Autumn figured there had to be several women clamoring to spend time with him while he was back in town. The orchids he'd sent earlier in the week were beautiful and quite unexpected. Even the handwritten card had been a surprise considering how they'd left things. Remembering the words made her smile.

I saw these and immediately thought of you. They're striking, but they don't compare to your beauty.

The degree in which his words affected her was surprising. Autumn was regretting having had Jenna thank him on her behalf when she'd called to give him an update on how things had been going. A bit petty but considering the last words she'd delivered at the time, Autumn deemed it appropriate.

They exited the elevator and were making their way through the stadium when Autumn heard a baritone voice calling out her name. She stopped and turned to find a tall, handsome man wearing black dress slacks and a black polo style shirt with the Blackhawks logo on the breast pocket, heading in her direction.

"Hmm, he's a cutie. Who is he?" Jenna asked.

"Edward Lewis." Surprise brightened her eyes. "He's an old friend."

"Autumn Knight, I thought that was you." He pulled her into his arms for a big hug.

"Edward." She immediately stepped out of his hold for reasons she didn't want to explore. Having another man's arms around her felt...wrong. "How are you?"

"I'm good, and you?"

Jenna cleared her throat. "Sorry, Edward, this is my friend and assistant, Jenna Lowe."

"Nice to meet you," she replied, offering him a quick wave.

"So, you work for the Blackhawks now," Autumn gestured at his shirt.

"Yes—"

"What do you do?" Jenna asked, giving him the once-over.

"I'm the new team physical therapist," he replied before turning his attention back to Autumn. "Looks like you're heading out—"

"You married?"

"Jenna..." Autumn gave her friend the evil eye.

Edward laughed. "Not yet." He smiled at both women. "I'm engaged to an amazing woman. She's a nurse."

Jenna's face brightened. "Me too, the engaged part," she flashed her engagement ring. "My boo is a chemical engineer."

"Congratulations," he said, smiling. "And how about you Autumn, are you married?"

"Have a good weekend, ladies, see you next week," a couple of staff members said as they headed for the exit. Both women smiled and nodded.

Autumn raised her left hand and wiggled her ring finger. "Nope, still single."

He smirked. "I was sure that your father would have married you off to the perfect guy by now," he stated. "He certainly didn't think I was that person."

Jenna's phone blasted, a familiar tone—Happy. After checking the screen, she said, "Here's my baby now. Excuse me for a second." She stepped away to take the call.

"What did you mean by that comment Edward?"

"Nothing."

"You and I both know there's something. Spill…"

"It's just, your dad made it clear to me," he sneered. "And anyone else he thought was interested in you, that we shouldn't waste our time. He had big plans for his only daughter, and he wasn't going to let little school crushes interfere with your big and bright future," he explained. "When he didn't think I received his message, he sent his bodyguards around to make sure I did. And I'm good, but I couldn't take on six of them. So, I never contacted you again."

Autumn gritted her teeth as she tried to control her anger. She knew her father had been protective, domineering, and even tried to encourage her to date men he picked for her over the years, but she never expected that he was actively sabotaging her social life. Why shouldn't she, though. Her father made his intentions for Autumn clear her entire life. The man was relentless in his pursuit of what he thought was best.

Jenna walked up to Autumn and Edward. "After I hung up with Jackson, Sally called. The girls are waiting for us."

"Please don't let me keep you two from your friends. It was good seeing you, Autumn. Take care of yourself, and I'm sure we'll see each other around."

"I'm sure we will. Have a good weekend." Both women watched as he walked away.

"So, what did I miss?" Jenna asked.

"Edward just confirmed what I've always suspected about my father and his meddling in my private life."

"So, you and the fine therapist dated?"

Autumn's mouth curved into a smile. "Briefly, when I came home for summer break, my junior year of college."

Jenna tilted her head and placed her hands on her hips. "Let me guess. He dumped you for someone else. No, worse, he cheated on you."

Autumn watched as Jenna's lips drew back in a snarl. "Calm down, it wasn't like that, he just kind of ghosted."

"What do you mean, kind of?"

She adjusted her purse strap on her shoulder and started walking. "After our third date, when I thought I'd let Edward get to second base, he told me that he was going to be too busy to hang out anymore. That he'd gotten a summer job."

"That's understandable," Jenna replied.

"Yes, it is." Autumn nodded slowly. "Especially since he went to work for one of my father's *preferred* orthopedics. I guess it was my father's way of thanking him for backing off. Truthfully, it wasn't the first time something like that had happened."

Jenna stopped short. "Seriously?" Her eyebrows stood at attention.

"Seriously. I guess my father's job offer was bigger than my boobs. Let's go. I could use a drink."

CHAPTER 17

Grant settled in his chair at the desk, a beautiful seventy-nine-inch walnut and granite work of art given to him by another satisfied customer signing the last set of contracts that required his attention. He laid down his pen and stretched out his arms. Grant had attended more meetings than he'd counted on and was ready to call it a day. He had long since removed the gray Armani suit jacket and tie, unbuttoned his shirt's top buttons, and now it was time for a drink.

He stood and moved to the bar in the corner of his office. After pulling down a glass and filling it with a few ice cubes, he poured his favorite spirit, the Pappy Van Winkle Family Reserve. Grant swirled his glass allowing the ice to cool the gold substance before taking a sip. He raised the glass to his lips when his office door opened.

"Drinking without me, son?"

Grant smiled as he watched his uncle enter the room. The man looked better than he had in ages. His grey suit made of tweed fabric, tailored to fit and accented with red buttons, made Grant smile. It was so him. Grant placed his glass down on the bar, walked over and hugged him.

"That depends. Are you allowed to have a drink?"

"Of course, I am, especially when I have a win to share." He took the chair closest to the door that sat across from his nephew's desk.

Grant and his uncle often shared a drink at the end of the week, where they would share their wins and losses. They would celebrate the positive outcomes or work to resolve whatever problems they may have encountered. By the wide smile Ben was gifting him; Grant figured it had to be one hell of a win. He returned to the bar, grabbed another glass and poured. Grant picked up both glasses and took the chair next to Ben.

"Here you go," he handed him the drink. "Neat."

"Thank you."

"First things first uncle, where's Sam?"

"He'll be back to get me in about thirty minutes," he stated before taking a sip of his drink. "I told him I wanted to see you alone before we head home."

Grant sat back in his chair. "Now, what's your win for the day?" He brought his glass to his lips and took a drink.

"How about you go first son," his uncle encouraged, taking another sip from his glass.

Grant heaved a sigh thinking his uncle might be stalling because he actually had bad news to share, but because he'd said his news was a win, Grant relaxed and started with the good news about all the progress made at both the United Center and the Castle. Uncle Ben clearly explained how proud he was of all his nephew's accomplishments.

"Your turn."

"We got the last of my test results back and…" he raised his glass, took another drink while eyeing him over the rim. Ben had a flair for the dramatic.

"And." Grant sat forward in his chair as his heart raced.

"All is well, son," Ben announced proudly, grinning from ear-to-ear. "The scans were clear."

Grant fought back tears. Losing his parents at such a young age had been difficult, and he was thankful his uncle had stepped up and took care of him. Now Grant was very thankful that he didn't have to relive such anguish again. To think it might not have happened. His mind flashed back to the day everything changed.

"Where did this come from?" Felicia Blake demanded.

"I'm not a liberty to say," Jai answered, turning his gaze toward Grant, who stood near the olive-skinned beauty, tightlipped, but his expression concerned.

Dr. Felicia Blake, a former CIA medical research scientist, specializing in biochemistry who was Deputy Director of the CDC, was Meek's sister-in-law, one-third of identical triplets, and heir to her family's billion-dollar international security firm.

"If you want my help with this, I need to know. This ..." she gestured toward the serum. "This isn't like anything that I've ever seen. Where the hell did it come from?"

Grant moved forward, clasping a hand on Jai's shoulder. "The Castle's medical facility has access to medicines and treatments that aren't anywhere close to being on the market yet. The FDA will not approve these types of serums."

"Why?" she snapped, putting her eyes back on the eyepiece of the microscope. "Do you know how many people can be healed from this alone?"

Jai shared an uneasy glance with Grant.

"Yes," Jai said. "But that's not how money is made here in America."

Felicia lifted her head and parted her lips to protest, but Jai held up a hand and continued. "You know as well as I do that money isn't made on curing a disease. It's in the research, development, and treatment. If diseases were cured at the onset, then the money train stops there. Companies can't make billions that way."

"You have to publish your findings on this," she said, shaking her head. "You can't keep this to yourself. I can't keep this from the public."

"You can, if you want to live," Jai warned.

"Are you threatening me?" She frowned, taking a step back.

"Not at all," Grant interjected. "You know people have killed for less. You mess with their money, and they will take it out on you. They'll try to destroy you ... destroy us. You know that this business is ruthless."

Felicia lowered her gaze to the tiles. "I can see the truth in that, but it's so hard to let others suffer when ..."

"I know," Jai said, placing a steadying hand over hers. "And in time, we'll find a way to filter this into the industry, but in a way that means we won't be put under scrutiny."

"And no one will lose their lives in the process," Grant said. "For now, though, I need you to validate the chemical compound of this serum so it can be administered to my uncle, and it will save his life. Chemo is not working, and it's draining the life out of him. If this treatment can do what Jai claims, then it's worth a try. I owe that man my life. And I'd like for him to live out the rest of it with the love of his life, and in the best health possible."

"Please help us," Jai said. "This needs to be transformed into a dosage that won't overpower him, and it still can undo the effects of the chemo."

Felicia looked at the purple liquid in the vial. "You know, folks always wondered how Magic Johnson was able to live out with his HIV status when so many others died off during that time." She glanced up at Jai. "He received something like this from overseas?"

"There's always been speculation," Jai answered. "Only he, his wife, and his physician know for sure."

"And that's another thing." Felicia began to pace the length of the room. "How are you going to explain his miraculous recovery to his oncologist? That man knows Ben Khambrel is at death's door."

"We don't explain anything," Grant answered, taking a seat on the chair near the silver research table. "I've had all of his medical records transferred to Jai. He'll be overseeing my uncle's care from this point forward."

"All the bases covered, eh?" she said with a laugh. "I'll do it, but I want access to some of the other research in this place. And I want to be a part of the team when you're filtering some of these treatments into the medical world."

Jai sighed, his shoulders lowered as though weighed down in defeat.

"If you want my help, I'm going to want in, bottom line." Her chin lifted as her chest heaved in an effort to hold in her emotions.

Grant put his hand on Jai's. "Brother, I know you don't want this facility's power put on the map, but this is my uncle's life we're talking about. The longer we wait, the more her suffers. I want his pain to end."

Jai shook his head. "And it will. From what I've seen of this serum, it will bring something close to immediate results."

"Jai, let's get started with Ben's treatment," Felicia said in a resigned whisper, putting her fight for inclusion to the side. At least

for the moment.

"Thank you, and I promise we'll work out everything else to the benefit of everyone involved. It'll mean you might have to be here in Chicago to make that happen."

"How will your husband feel about that?" Grant asked.

"Griffin will support me all the way down the line," she replied. "But for now, let me get on this. It's going to take a few hours"

"Ben's on his way here and I'll get him settled in the Lincoln Park suite of the Castle." Grant paused a minute. "Is it possible that whatever treatment you're going to administer can be done in the comfort of one of the master bedrooms there, rather than this facility? He's been in enough places like this."

The Castle's clinic rooms were nicely decorated but there was no mistaking the surroundings. The large leather reclining chairs were comfortable, but no matter how lovely the environment, the pole holding the life-saving medicine going through his veins and state of the art equipment screamed clinical. But this place held a world of secrets. So much so, that Dr. Randall Fowler, the director prior to Jai's taking over, had to carried out of the place by security. He was screaming that they would pay for what they'd done. And that there were people higher up than them who would take them out. Jai was still trying to figure out what Dr. Fowler meant.

"I can make that happen," she said, smiling. Then she waved her hand in a shooing motion. "Now get out. I have work to do."

"That's great news," Grant said, fighting back his emotions. "Just great." His uncle reached for his hand, gave it a squeeze, and a sense of relief washed over him.

"So, how are things going with your lady?"

Grant laughed. "She's not my lady." *Not yet.*

"Not yet," Sam said as though reading Grant's thoughts.

"There have been a few complications that we will need to work out, but I'm pretty confident that we'll get through it." Grant finished off his drink.

"I hope so, son. Everyone should have the opportunity to find their one great love."

"Is Sam your great love, uncle?"

"I better be," Sam declared as he walked in the office dressed in a suit similar to the one his uncle wore, only his was black. Grant found it funny, but sweet at how they enjoyed dressing alike.

Uncle Ben stood, and the two men embraced. "You're back."

"I'm back." Sam turned his attention to Grant, and the two hugged. "How are you?"

"I'm great now."

Sam smiled. "He told you the good news."

"He sure did." Grant nodded.

Sam looked down at the empty glass sitting on the desk in front of Uncle Ben. "Looks like I got back just in time too."

Grant pointed at his uncle and like a tattle-telling child and said, "He told me he could have one drink."

"Snitch," he whispered, laughing.

"I'm sure he did," Sam glared at Ben. "It's fine, but no nightcap before bed for you, mister."

"Fine, no nightcap." He turned his attention to Grant. "I guess we should head home. I am a bit tired."

"Wait," Grant raised his hand. "You didn't say. Are you done with all the treatments?"

"Yes, I'm done. I have supplements that I'll need to continue taking, but Dr. Maharaj and Dr. Blake said I'm in full remission. They'll want to take some bloodwork every six months, but Dr. Maharaj gave me supplements—not medicine, and he put me on a diet plan that removes pork completely from my meal choices. Only organically raised beef, chicken and fish. A great deal of raw, healthy vegetables."

Grant nodded, too overwhelmed to speak. He was thankful that Jai had facilitated the treatments that were not available to everyone in the States.

"But he didn't say I couldn't have a little libation every day. In fact, he encouraged it. Manichevetz, especially."

"Well, that's not Manichevetz," Sam said, giving Ben the evil eye. "That's the sweet red wine they used to serve at communion."

"No, this is not, but it's a distant cousin. Bottoms up." He polished off the last of the drink and placed the glass on the desk.

Grant couldn't help but laugh.

All three men headed for the door.

"Give me a minute Sam."

"Sure, I'll wait by the elevator."

Uncle Ben turned to Grant. "You asked if Sam was my great love. Yes, he is, but he wasn't my first love. We both know that you've never experienced either one." He patted Grant on the cheek. "If you're lucky enough to find someone who's both son, don't let her go."

"Thanks." He watched as his uncle made it to the elevator.

Grant returned to his desk, feeling more than relieved that his uncle was going to be all right. He owed Jaidev Maharaj big time and he would be forever grateful to his king brother for putting himself and the Castle at risk by bringing Felicia Blake in to help.

He started collecting his thing when his cell phone rang. Grant read the name, placed the call on speaker and answered, "Dro, what's up?"

"I have Vikkas on the line."

"Hey Vik."

"Greetings."

"We've got a problem, man," Dro said.

"Another one?" He stood with his arms crossed at his chest.

"One of my people working in the village of Wilmette heard a rumor about an injunction coming our way."

"An injunction, why?" Grant dropped his arms, leaned forward using his hands to brace himself.

"Something about the Castle. It seems someone is claiming the property is sitting on or is part of a historical landmark."

"Son-of-a-bitch." Grant lowered his head and stared at the phone as if he could see Dro through the line. "When I first made it to town a reporter caught me leaving the hotel and asked me about a rumor she'd heard."

"What kind of rumor?"

"She said someone was coming for the Castle. At the time I didn't think anything about it. Especially since she...."

"What ... she what, Grant?" Vikkas prompted.

"She hit on me and when I didn't bite, that was when she mentioned the rumor," he explained.

"I get that, and since you and Vikkas are the Kings responsible for untangling all of the Castle's property issues, I figured you'd know what to do first."

Grant dropped down in his chair. "I'll see what I can find out."

CHAPTER 18

Standing in the middle of the newly renovated game room located in the Castle, brought on a smile because it was now Grant's favorite room. Having received and entertained everything on his brother Kings' wish list, the room hosted beautiful views, a large wood fireplace, multiple types of leather and cloth seating, and various levels and styles of table settings. The two pool tables, pinball and gaming machines, poker tables, and several bars stocked with top-shelf alcohol were a big hit. The expensive artwork painted by Temple Maharaj decorating the walls completed the contemporary look of the room.

Grant gazed out of the cathedral windows at the exquisite view of the gardens and the Castle grounds, wishing he could share the experience with Autumn. Three weeks had passed, and Grant hadn't shared more than a handful of words with the woman who was constantly invading his thoughts and dreams. Finding out who was behind all his troubles was taking longer than he would like.

The catered lunches, flowers and massage therapy sessions he gifted her after he returned to Texas for business had little effect since she sent her thanks through his co-conspirator, Jenna.

Together they would figure out which claims were valid.

He had come to the castle to survey the grounds and take note of the areas that were mentioned in the injunction that Dro managed to get his hands on before the process server had delivered it to all of the parties named on the Motion. He spoke with Khalil and had found out that the Castle itself started with a bridge and meadow. Vikkas was digging into the Historical Society's assertions. Surrounding buildings were painstakingly built under Khalil's directive to mirror an already existing structure – The Baha'i Temple.

Grant's cell rang. "Khambrel."

"Check your email," Meeks ordered in a tone which told Grant he wasn't going to like what he found.

He put the call on speaker and complied. "What am I looking for?"

"Robert just sent you a video."

"Got it, what is this?"

"Surveillance from the Zürich bank. Check out the woman in the white sun hat," Meeks directed.

Grant focused on the semi blurred face and asked, "Who is she?"

"According to the sign-in sheet at the bank and documentation she presented, she's Autumn Knight," Meeks explained.

"She's clearly not Autumn Knight," Grant said, relief washed over him like a much needed and relaxing shower. "The woman is blonde and white."

"We know, but do you recognize her from anywhere?"

"No, but this clears Autumn, right?" He didn't even try to hide his excitement. "Not to mention her background check came up clean as well," he reminded Meeks.

"Yes, of course, but we can't say for certain that she knows nothing about her father's business endeavors. It might be time for you two to talk," he suggested.

"I agree, but …"

"But what? You've been protesting her innocence for weeks now. What's holding you back? Have you changed your mind about her or something?"

"Of course not, it's just we have no real proof of anything." Grant took a seat at the bar. "Her name is on a number of bank accounts with a ton of dirty money, man," he reminded his friend.

"Yeah, but her father is using someone to impersonate her to hide his dirty money."

"Autumn could be implicated and that could destroy her reputation before everything was sorted out. Not to mention kill any chance of a future we might have." Grant heaved a sigh. "If I tell her what we suspect without anything to back it up, she might not believe me."

"Even if it could clear her name?"

"No, she doesn't realize her name needs to be cleared. It's bad enough I didn't tell her the truth about myself from the beginning. She's never going to trust me."

"You don't know that for sure."

"We're accusing her father of using her as a part of his criminal enterprise without her knowledge." He fisted his hand and pounded it on the table. "The man's still her father, Meeks. If I'm going lay that at her feet, I need tangible and credible proof."

"Look, we have statements from three of the hotel blackmail victims."

Grant rolled his neck trying to work out the angry crook.

"The identical blackmail amount was deposited into her father's account, an account he put her name on, remember? We even have a copy of the signature card from the bank and compared it to her actual signature from your contract with UC. It's not hers."

An even bigger sense of relief washed over Grant. Meeks was right, and while his instinct to protect Autumn had kicked in, her loyalty to her father concerned him immensely.

"If nothing else man, she at least deserves to know what her father's been up to. That way when it all comes falling down, she won't be surprised, and she'll have a parachute."

"Parachute?"

"Yes, you."

Grant took a moment to absorb that information. "You're right. I'll talk to Autumn."

"Good. Any word from Daron yet?"

Grant stood and stretched, reminding himself to get in a workout before the day was over. "Yes, he's on the way now to give me an update."

"Let me know if you need anything from me."

"Will do." Grant ended the call. He moved around the bar, picked up a crystal decanter, then resisted the urge to pour himself a glass of twenty-five-year-old single malt scotch. Thoughts of Autumn helped fight back his anxiousness while waiting for Daron to arrive.

"You might want to hold off before taking another drink. You're going to need a clear head," Daron stated in a harsh tone as he entered the room. He was dressed in black jeans, t-shirt, and combat boots. His look seemed to match his mood and mirrored Grant's look and attitude.

Grant turned and accepted Daron's outstretched hand. "Thanks for getting here so fast."

"No sweat." He took a seat at the bar and scanned the room. "Man, I can't get over how cool this room looks now."

Grant nodded, and he rubbed his cheek. "It has everything everyone wanted."

Daron looked over his shoulder. "Even the top shelf alcohol."

"Want a drink?"

"Later. A former lieutenant I knew from back in the day picked up something."

Grant took a seat on the barstool next to Daron. "What?"

"Your uncle borrowed money from an old G named Jimmy G."

He still couldn't believe his uncle knew people who were considered old gangsters. The kind that ran the underbelly of most cities back in the day. Benjamin Khambrel was as straight as they came. Well, except his love life. "Yeah, I know, and I paid him back in full. Including the outrageous vigorish he charged, the crooked bastard."

Daron nodded like a bobble doll. "Outrageous interest comes with the territory when you deal with loan sharks."

"He got paid, and I have my uncle's marker back. There is no proof that anything transpired between him and my uncle. Why is he coming for me now?" Grant asked with a deep frown.

Daron reached for his beeping phone. "That's just it. He's not coming for you. But—"

"But he knows who is?"

"He knows how to find out who is, but it's going to cost us," he replied, keeping his eyes on his phone, reading an incoming message.

"Us, and how much?"

Daron placed his phone back on his hip. "Twenty grand and a favor."

"A favor?"

"Affirmative, but the favor is on my tab," Daron stated without providing any additional details.

"Hell no." Grant shook his head. It was bad enough he had to deal with this craziness. He wasn't pulling his brother into any more than necessary. He pointed to himself. "This is on me."

Daron crossed his arms at his chest. "That's not how things work in Chi-town. Besides, you don't have anything he wants."

"What does he want?"

Daron shook his head. "That's between me and my source."

"I can't put you out like that man."

"You're not, unless you don't pay me back that money." He raised an eyebrow.

Grant stood and walked behind the bar. "So, you paid already? He bent down, opened the cabinet, pushed away a false wall to reveal a safe. He keyed in a code, opened the door, and pulled out two stacks of hundred-dollar bills from one of the nine shelves inside. After they accepted the managing member status, each king had placed in a disposable amount of cash.

"Of course, I did." Daron grinned and presented his palms. "When an opportunity presents itself, you have to move quickly."

Grant closed the safe, came from around the bar, stood in front of his brother, and handed him the cash. "There goes my poker money."

"It's not like you were going to win against Reno anyway," he said, shrugging.

Grant smirked. "Thanks man, I appreciate it."

"No problem, we should have something in a few days."

He walked back around the bar. "Now, do you want that drink?"

"Yes."

Grant pulled out another glass and poured two shots in each. He handed a glass to Daron, raised his, and said, "To finding answers."

"Answers," Daron agreed, before touching his glass to Grant's.

He gritted his teeth, responding to the liquid fire making its way through his system. "Let me ask you something."

"Sure."

"Do you think Alderman Knight could have anything to do with this?" Grant leaned against the bar

"The alderman is dirty, without a doubt," Daron replied, crossing one leg over the other. "But this is an area he knows better than to venture into."

"Are you going to be okay stepping back into that world?"

Daron stood, picked up his glass and tossed back the last of his drink. "I haven't. I promised Cameron that I was done, and I am. I just happen to have contacts who straddle both worlds. I'm good, no worries." He pulled out his keys. "My question to you is, what will you do when you have your answers and you find *your* enemy?"

Grant's lips drew back in a snarl. "I guess we'll see."

"I guess we will." Daron turned to leave when Grant stopped him.

"Before you go. I'm hearing rumblings about some type of injunction against the Castle."

"What the hell?" He pulled out his cell and started dialing. "Have you talked to Khalil or Vikkas about this yet? What about the other Kings?"

"Hold up, man." Grant held up his hand. "Let's not get everyone riled up yet. I need you to do some recon on the members of the Wilmette Historical Society." He texted Daron the list of names. "Someone put them up to this."

Daron sighed and placed his cell in his pocket. "Fine, but once I found out what you asked for, you have to call a meeting to tell everyone. We're all in this together remember?"

"I remember," Grant acknowledged nodding. "Whoever's trying to come for the Kings of the Castle will have one hell of a fight on their hands."

CHAPTER 19

Autumn was spending another Friday night alone at home in her fully restored Lincoln Park brownstone. The place was situated in the quiet, upscale neighborhood on a tree-lined street.

Bringing the glass of white Moscato to her lips, she inhaled its fruity aroma before taking a sip, Autumn glanced around her home and smiled. She'd gotten the place at auction for a steal and was very pleased with the final outcome. It had taken over two years and a large chunk of her savings to find the perfect marriage between old charm and modern luxury.

The four-level property not only featured four large bedrooms with ensuite bathrooms, including a master suite on its own level, the main floor had a full-size living area with a wood fireplace and dining room that would seat twelve. The mixture of antique and contemporary furnishings made the place hers. The professional kitchen, private second-floor deck, nice yard, and fully equipped home theater and game room made her place perfect for entertaining. Fat chance, since she was striking out in the relationship department. Now she understood why almost every single prospect had disappeared before any chance for a real relationship materialized.

She parked on the sofa and reached for the television remote when her doorbell rang. Autumn looked at the clock on her fireplace mantel. The only person who would be coming by this late without calling was her father. She finished off the last of her wine and placed the glass on the table. Autumn walked to the door, opened the brass peephole she'd had installed on the large oak wood door, and peered out.

Autumn's heart raced, and her breath caught in her throat, and she froze. It was as if she'd been zapped by a taser gun. Grant Khambrel was standing on her porch dressed casually in black jeans, a black button-down shirt, and sports jacket. He looked as though he just stepped off the cover of *GQ*. Autumn felt like one of those volcanoes she enjoyed reading about—hot lava racing through her veins settling between her thighs and ready to erupt.

The bell rang again, breaking her trance and without thinking she opened the door. "Grant," she greeted in a raspy whisper.

A guttural growl escaped Grant's throat as he eyed her from head to toe. Autumn felt his heated glare and saw his eyes dilate. His gaze roamed her body again as she finally realized why. Autumn forgot she was wearing a burgundy lace trimmed sheer baby doll nightgown and matching robe. She loved wearing sexy lingerie, even if it was just for herself.

* * *

Grant had never felt desire so strong in his entire life. His heart was beating so fast he couldn't believe he was still standing. The need to have this woman, to make her his, was overwhelming. Then it suddenly hit him, what if she wasn't alone? His passion turned to anger so fast it scared him. His hands fisted at his sides.

"Have I interrupted anything?" he asked, his jaw clenched.

Autumn tightened the robe about her waist and crossed her arms at the chest. "Not that it's any of your business, but no. I'm alone."

"Dressed like that?"

She narrowed those piercing green eyes. "Yes."

Grant's body relaxed instantly. "Good." His eyes took in their fill again, and the corners of his mouth turned up.

"I'd ask how you knew where I lived, but I can guess."

"I don't think you can, and no, it wasn't Jenna who told me." He slid his hands into his pants pockets. "May I come in?"

"Why?" She lowered her arms and placed both hands on her hips. "With the exception of a few quick business meetings before you up and left town, I haven't seen you in weeks."

He leaned onto the door jamb and intertwined his fingers, dropping them at his waist. Autumn evidently wanted answers before they went one step further. That was fine with him. "You're the one who wanted to keep things professional, remember?"

Her tone softened as she said, "True, but then you sent all those sweet, beautiful, and thoughtful gifts."

Grant nodded. "The ones you had Jenna thank me for instead of picking up the phone yourself."

Autumn sighed and lowered her hands. She looked up and met his stare. "What do you want, Grant?"

He straightened his stance. "Let me in and I'll tell you."

Autumn took several steps back. Grant crossed the threshold, closed and locked the door behind him.

"What I want, Autumn Knight, is you." He closed the distance between them.

"You could've fooled me," she whispered, fidgeting with her robe.

"I guess it's time that I prove it." Grant ran the back of his hand down the side of her face, and she trembled. His fingers lightly touched her lips, and he felt the breath she exhaled, and it pleased him immensely knowing he'd elicited such a response. He cupped Autumn's face with both hands. "You're the most intelligent, witty, awesome, passionate, and beautiful woman I've ever seen, and I've missed you like crazy." He leaned down and ran his tongue across her lips before kissing her gently.

"I've missed you too," Autumn admitted against his mouth.

Grant captured her mouth in a passionate and possessive kiss. Their tongues mated as if they were meant for each other. Autumn went up on her toes and circled her arms around Grant's neck. His hands loosened the loop on her robe and wrapped his arms around her waist, pulling her into his body. He wanted her to feel how much he desired her, and he knew she received the message when she moaned in his mouth. Grant slid his mouth across her cheek, jawline, and down her neck where he licked and sucked hard leaving his mark.

He raised his head and stared into her desire-filled eyes. "If you want me to stop, tell me now." He ran his tongue across her lips.

Autumn pulled his head back down to hers and devoured his mouth, giving him the answer he needed. He lifted her off her feet and asked, "Where's the bedroom?"

"Second floor," she responded without hesitation.

Grant carried Autumn up the stairs, kissing her along the way as he walked through an open set of double doors. A small tableside lamp, along with the moonlight shining through her bowed windows, illuminated the room. His eyes zeroed in on the dark gray California

King platform bed that sat against a light gray and white reclaimed wood wall. Grant barely noticed the sitting area in front of the window or the stone fireplace in the corner. He was too busy concentrating on the woman in his arms.

He placed Autumn on her feet next to the bed and took a step back wanting to enjoy the view. Autumn's breasts were full and perfect, her stomach flat, waist small flaring out to a round behind that all had him hard as concrete.

"Take off your robe," Grant said, his tone husky.

Autumn smiled, ready to do his bidding, but then she said, "Before I do, I have to tell you something."

Seeing how her breathing had escalated and the way her hands slightly shook, he knew she was nervous, but why? "Okay."

"It's been a while since I've done this," she confessed, her cheeks turning the bright color of pink.

"How long is a while?" He couldn't hide the surprise in his voice or on his face.

"I'm not a virgin. At least, I don't think so."

She didn't think so? What the hell. "Excuse me?"

"The first and last time I had sex was in high school. By the time things got started, it was over. When I talked to my girlfriends about my experience, and they told me about their first times, it was nothing like mine." She shrugged. "Mine wasn't even painful."

Grant bet he knew why, too. The dumb kid didn't know what he was doing or what he was fortunate enough to have, either. Autumn had more passion in her small finger than most women he knew. The stupid guy probably hadn't even broken her hymen. Autumn was a twenty-eight-year-old virgin and didn't even realize.

Well her status was about to change.

He reached for Autumn's hands, brought her wrists to his nose, and inhaled them before kissing her palms. "After tonight, sweetheart, there won't be any doubt about what you are, that I promise. "

"And what will I be?" she whispered.

Mine. "A very satisfied woman," he answered. "Now, about that, robe."

She smiled and rolled her shoulders back letting the garment fall to the floor. Grant's eyes widened, and his tongue darted across his lips. Autumn's nipples were taut, her lace thong was damp and adhered to her plump folds, and her womanly scent enticed him. He was ravenous for Autumn, but he had to control his wolfish side for now.

"Take that off," he growled as he began peeling off his shirt. He removed his shoes and socks before sliding out of his pants.

Autumn removed her gown and thong, letting them pool on the floor with her robe. Her nervousness must have gotten the best of her because she immediately went to the bed and slid under the paisley comforter.

"You can't hide from me Autumn," Grant announced, lowering his boxer-briefs, exposing his large and thick shaft that he quickly encased in a condom he'd pulled out of his wallet.

"I'm not…hiding. I'm…cold." Autumn shuddered as if to prove that point.

Grant joined her on the bed. "Soon, you won't be that I can promise."

"Promise?"

"Promise." He captured her mouth in a deep passionate kiss. "It's time that I make you mine."

CHAPTER 20

His…

Autumn felt pleasure unlike anything she'd ever known. Their hungry kisses had her body demanding more. Moans and words like *please* and *now* escaped her lips. She didn't recognize her voice. Grant sucked, bit, and pulled on her nipples. Autumn felt like a fuse had been lit inside of her, and she was about to take off like a rocket.

Grant ran his hand down her stomach, and his finger slid through the fine wet hairs that covered her womanly mound until he slid first one, then a second finger inside, with a third on her pearl, stroking Autumn until that fuse he'd lit finally exploded.

"Grant," she screamed.

"That's it, come for me, baby," he crooned. Damn, so wet."

"Oh yes, yes," she cried out, making powerful thrust against his fingers that fueled her desire.

Grant slid down her body and placed her legs over his shoulders. "Now, for my taste."

"Taste?" she whispered.

Grant knew this would be a new experience for her, and he couldn't wait to see and feel her response. He slid his tongue up and down then between her folds as if he was trying to lick her clean.

Grant gripped her thighs tight with both hands keeping them flat on the bed and pushed his tongue deep inside of Autumn's core. She shivered and began moving her hips to the tempo he set and then quickly fell apart.

"Grant!"

He held his mouth to her until those shivers ended. Grant kissed and licked his way up her body, leaving marks in his wake until he captured her mouth. "That's you, baby, on my tongue. And you taste so damn sweet. But I need to be inside you."

"Yes, please."

"You're tight, baby, so this might be a bit uncomfortable at first. I'll take it slow," he promised gazing into Autumn's eyes as he inched inside.

Grant had to call upon all his strengths and will power to hold back the beast that wanted freedom; the part of him that knew Autumn would be the only one that could ever fully satisfy his every need. He gently kissed her when he felt that barrier. "Ready?"

"Yes."

Grant inched forward, and Autumn gasped and gripped the bed sheets

"Are you all right, baby?" He remained still giving her body time to adjust to his size and the invasion.

"Yes," she whimpered. Autumn quieted herself few moments, then began rotating her hips beneath him, and Grant knew she was truly ready. He moved in and out of her body, but no matter how slow he tried to go, Autumn wasn't having it.

"More," she pleaded, holding his gaze. "Don't hold back."

Grant sucked on Autumn's tongue, neck, arms, and breasts, feasting on her body like a starving man at an open buffet. Grant increased his rhythm, enjoying her willing luscious body.

Autumn had never experienced anything like the feeling of joining with Grant. She could feel the throb of his desire with each forceful plunge. Autumn dug her nails in his shoulder, licking and biting his skin leaving her own marks. She wrapped her legs around his back and raised her hips with each deep driving force that pushed her over the edge.

They reached the pinnacle of satisfaction together.

"Grant!"

"Autumn!"

They remained connected until the tremors eased. Much later, Grant finally slipped out of Autumn, rolled off her and gathered her into his arms, both trying to catch their breath.

"That was incredible," Grant rolled onto his side, propped up his head, and smiled down at her. "How do you feel, sweetheart?"

She smiled at the term of endearment he'd used and said, "Like a live wire. Every inch of my body is on alert. What we just did is nothing like what happened to me before."

Grant laughed. "I hate to break it to you, baby, but you were still a virgin."

"I know." Autumn covered her face with both hands and shook her head.

"Don't hide from me." He pulled down her hands and kissed her. "I'll be right back."

Autumn watched Grant ease out of the bed and walk naked into the bathroom. "Wow, that was truly remarkable. Too bad I won't ever be able to walk again."

Soon the water streamed into her tub, and she sat up slowly, trying to regain her bearing.

Grant walked out the bathroom in all his glorious nakedness, and Autumn's body stirred with need. "I love that vintage claw foot tub. I've never seen one so big."

"Neither have I." Her eyes roamed his body and she gave him a Cheshire cat smile.

Grant gifted her with a wide smile of his own. "I was referring to the tub, but thank you."

"Thank you. Each bathroom has a unique tub, and they're all made to fit two people. All my bedrooms have a distinctive story. If you're nice to me, I might tell you a few."

"Nice." Grant laughed, scooped Autumn up and carried her into the bathroom. "You need to soak. It'll help with the soreness." He gently lowered her into the warm soapy water.

"This is perfect," she moaned. "And it feels divine."

"That's good to hear. I found everything for the bath on the counter."

Autumn smiled up at him. "You didn't have to do this, but thank you, Grant."

His mouth curved into a smile, and he ran the back of his hand down the side of her face before he leaned over and gently kissed her on the lips. "You are so very beautiful."

"Are you going to stay the night?"

"I was hoping you'd want me to, especially since we're just getting started."

CHAPTER 21

After Autumn's bath and Grant took a quick shower, he kept his word. They had spent the next few hours making love and exploring all the delicacies that their bodies could handle. Now he was looking down into the face of the stunning woman who was fast asleep in his arms. Even after the unprecedented level of passion they'd experienced, Grant still wanted more.

She was strong and independent which he admired, but when Autumn was in his arms, she became submissive to her needs and desires, almost his equal in giving and receiving pleasure the way they both craved.

Grant couldn't believe this was the same woman he had come to confront about her knowledge of her father's activities. He had wanted to discuss the situation and concerns in private, but when Autumn opened her door, dressed the way she was, his desire for her demolished all reasonable thought, and the last thing he wanted to do was talk about her father. His mind shut down and his desires took complete control.

* * *

Monday, Grant sat at the drafting table, trying to review plans for the center. Only his mind kept drifting back to the breathtaking woman with whom he'd shared an entire weekend. They spent Saturday and Sunday enjoying each other's company doing activities they both enjoyed—going to the museum, cooking together, and they even went to a place on the South side for some Chicago style stepping. They spent their nights making love, and Grant knew he wanted forever with Autumn. Unfortunately, there was still something hanging over their heads that could prevent that from happening.

A knock on the open door interrupted his musings before Mark walked into the office.

"Good morning," he said, pushing back thoughts of Autumn reaching for his coffee cup.

"Morning. We have a problem," he said frowning.

Grant was pleased that Mark had joined his team. He had become a valuable asset and Grant had even managed to convince him to accept the hefty salary that accompanied the position. "Have a seat and tell me what's up."

Mark settled in a chair across from Grant and said, "I received several calls this morning asking me to pull their names from my list of potential vendors for the United Center."

"Why?"

"They all gave me the same answer." He shook his head in frustration. "Now wasn't a good time to take on such a large project."

Grant's brows snapped together. "They *all* gave the same answer?" He set his cup down.

"Yeah, and we both know that's bull. Someone got to them, Grant, and they've been coached. I've heard that phrase tossed around before."

"But who?" Grant murmured, wondering if his mystery caller could have anything to do with this new development.

"Alderman Knight or one of his cronies." Mark's face twisted, and a vein popped out on his neck. "That man and anyone connected to all his wrongdoings should go to jail."

Grant knew he couldn't put it off any longer. He had to talk to Autumn. "Don't worry about it. We're working on something to loosen the alderman's hold on this community."

"I hope so." Mark stood, and Grant followed suit. "I better go, I'm meeting AJ at the lumberyard."

"I'm really glad you agreed to come on board. AJ speaks very highly of you."

"Yeah, she's pretty great too," he replied, his face reddened.

Grant knew when he'd met with his team last Friday for their weekly operational update meeting, the smiles and glances AJ and Mark shared when they thought no one was looking meant the two had made a significant connection. A lot like the connection he'd made with Autumn.

Only Grant was ready to take their relationship to the next level. First, he had to resolve the situation with her father once and for all.

"Before you go," Grant came from behind his desk and stood in front of Mark. "There's something I need you to look into for me."

"Sure thing, boss. What is it?"

"Excuse me, Grant. There's a gentleman here to see you, but he doesn't have an appointment. I think you have to see him," Jenna stated walking into the office, her mocha skin flushed with heat.

"I can come back," Mark stated, moving towards the door.

Jenna raised her hand stopping his progress. "Grant might want you to stay put."

Grant's brows drew together. "What's going on Jenna?"

"He's a server guy."

Grant's frown deepened. "A process server?"

She nodded. "That's what I said."

"How can you be sure?" Mark asked, gaze narrowing on her.

"I've seen him before. Just before that fraudulent slip and fall case began." She turned to Grant. "Should I bring him in?"

"Sure." Grant widened his stance and crossed his arms at his chest. He looked over to Mark. "That thing I wanted you to look into, I'm pretty sure this is it."

"Good afternoon, gentlemen," the short, balding, man wearing a brown suit said as he entered the room. "Which one of you is Mr. Grant Khambrel?"

"That would be me."

"Well this," he reached into his pocket and pulled out a letter size envelope. "Is for you."

He accepted and said, "Thanks."

"You've been served." The man turned and left the office.

Grant opened the envelope and pulled out the document. As he suspected, it was an injunction, but for what, exactly? He started reading through the document when he came upon the paragraph that was like a punch to the gut. He leaned against his desk.

"What's going on boss," Mark asked, concern clouded his features.

"This is an injunction preventing us from making any changes to or conducting any business on the property until the investigation or potential lawsuit gets settled," he stated as he kept reading. "All who used it as a residence, could remain in that part of the property for now."

"What?" Jenna dropped down in the chair sitting across from Grant's desk. "Someone is suing the United Center. You have to tell Autumn."

Grant looked up and saw panic on both Mark and Jenna's faces and the words he'd just spoke registered. "I'm sorry you guys. I was reading and thinking out loud. This," he held up the document. "Has nothing to do with the United Center. Everything's fine here, no worries." Grant straightened his stance and went and sat behind his desk. "This is Castle business."

Relief transformed their faces.

"Thank goodness. I'm sorry you have to deal with," she waved her hands toward the document. "Whatever that is, but I'm glad it doesn't have anything to do with this place. I have a wedding to pay for and I need my job."

"I completely understand. Do me a favor Jenna, keep this to yourself."

She nodded. "Sure, it's not my business. I'll be at my desk if you need anything."

Mark took the seat Jenna vacated and waited until she closed the door behind her before asking, "What do you need?"

"Thanks for the offer, but this is king business." He reached for the phone to call a meeting at Reno's place since it wasn't far from the Castle.

CHAPTER 22

Autumn couldn't stop smiling as she wrapped her lips around the straw and took a big pull of her chocolate shake made with Rocky Road ice cream. Another afternoon "pick me up" gift from Grant. He had ordered the delicious treat for everyone in the office and had it delivered. Grant was treating Autumn like a queen, his queen. No matter how hard she tried not to, Autumn had fallen head over heels in love with Grant Khambrel. The colorful print dress she was wearing matched her bright smile and attitude. It might be fall outside, but as far as she was concerned, it was Spring and Summer rolled together.

"Look at what just arrived." Jenna walked in the office carrying a large fruit bouquet. "First shakes and now fruit, what gives with your boy, Autumn?"

Before she could respond, Grant walked in, smiling. "I had to balance the snacks. Too much indulgence and no one would get any work done around here."

Autumn stopped breathing when Grant stepped over the threshold wearing a gray Italian suit that exemplified him as a man and king. She was hit by a wave of desire that had her gripping the desk to stay upright. Autumn took a quick breath and placed her drink on the desk.

"Thanks for the treats." His intense and heated gaze felt like a sweet caress.

"You're welcome. Can we talk?"

His tone and sudden demeanor were serious. Autumn hoped everything was all right. She would hate to think that he regretted their weekend together. "Sure."

"That's my cue." Jenna picked up the fruit and headed for the door. "I'll just keep this at my desk, I promise to save you some." She closed the door behind her.

Autumn came from around the desk and stood in front of it. "What's going on?"

Grant closed the short distance between them and pulled her into his arms. "I need to do this first." He brought his lips down to hers and devoured her mouth. Then those awesome hands were everywhere, and the kiss was almost desperate as though this was their last one.

"Wow." Her whole body was on alert and ready for whatever came next. Autumn leaned into Grant and felt his erection. He wanted her as much as she wanted him.

Grant laid his forehead against hers. "I didn't mean to lose control."

"I like it when we lose control." Her mouth curved into a sexy smile. "Why don't we tell Jenna not to disturb us, lock the door, and really lose control?"

* * *

"I'd love to, but we need to talk first." His expression closed up, and he released his hold, taking several steps back.

Autumn crossed her arms at her chest. "What is it?"

Grant's phone vibrated. He pulled it out of his pocket and checked the message. Daron needed to see him tonight.

"What is it, Grant?" He could hear the anxiety in her voice.

"I need to talk to you about your father."

"My father." She scowled and her body tensed. "What about him?"

"Are you aware of the financial stronghold your father has on this community?"

Autumn exhaled noisily. "I'm not involved in my father's business, Grant."

"But you are aware of his questionable and, in some instances, *illegal* business practices."

Autumn dropped her arms to her side and shrugged her shoulders. "Look, I know my father doesn't always walk the straight and narrow when it comes to business—"

"And you're okay with that?" Grant's head jerked back like he'd been shocked at the admission. "You're really okay with the fact that your father is taking advantage of his position as alderman?"

"I can't control what my father does. I love him in spite of what he does," her tone softened. "He's my father."

"That he is," he said, pacing the room. Autumn may not be defending him, but she wasn't condemning him either. That fact alone was annoying the hell out of Grant.

"What's he done now?" she asked, her voice weak with concern.

Grant stopped in his tracks, turned to face Autumn, and pushed his hands into his pockets. Time to hit her with some hard truths and lay his cards on the table. "Your father is blackmailing me and countless others."

He went on to explain in abundant detail everything they knew and suspected about the man she loved "in spite of what he does." Grant pulled up the email Robert sent him on his phone, showed her the surveillance video and the bank signature card with her name on it.

Confusion clouded her features, and she dropped down onto one of the chairs in front of her desk. "What is all of this? I don't understand any of it."

"Someone wants us to believe that you are in collusion with your father and sharing in his ill-gotten proceeds," he explained.

Understanding dawned on her face, and tears filled her eyes. "Is that what you think?" she whispered.

Grant pulled Autumn up out of the chair and into his arms. "Not for a second. You'd never cheat and steal from others. That's not who you are." He cupped her face with both hands and swiped away her tears with the pads of his thumbs, then held her gaze as he said, "I believe in you and us."

"Oh, Grant." She threw her arms around his neck and cried in his chest.

"Shhh, everything's going to be okay. I promise." Grant used his index finger to raise her face to meet his kiss—a kiss that was gentle and loving.

Autumn ended the kiss and whispered, "Thanks for believing in me."

"I know this may be a bad time to tell you this." Concern blossomed in Autumn's eyes which meant she was getting the wrong idea, and he had to alleviate her doubt. "I'm in love with you. I think I fell in love with you that day I saw you at the hospital. I hope *that's* not too creepy."

Autumn laughed. "That's not creepy at all. I love you too, Grant.

Not at first glance, but you kind of grew on me."

Grant leaned in for another kiss when his cell vibrated. "I have to get this baby."

Autumn nodded. She walked over to her desk, pulled out a Kleenex and wiped her eyes. "Yeah, Meeks, what's up?"

"Have you talked to Autumn yet?"

Grant's eyes lasered in on the woman he loved and who loved him back. He was besieged by emotions at the thought that such a beautiful and loving woman was his. "Yes, and she knows nothing about her father's business."

"I—"

"I believe her, man."

"So, do I," Meeks replied.

"You do?"

Autumn's attention snapped to him. He walked over to where she stood and pulled her into his arms.

"Yes. Ask Autumn if—"

"Ask her yourself," Grant said. "I'm putting you on speaker."

"You sure?" Grant heard the concern in his friend's voice.

"I'm sure, Meeks. No secrets," Grant insisted, placing the call on speaker. "Autumn Knight, this is Meeks Montgomery, my business partner, and friend. Go ahead, ask your question."

"Hello, Miss Knight, I hate we have to meet under these circumstances, but I need to ask you a question."

"Go ahead, and please, call me Autumn."

"Okay, Autumn, and I'm Meeks. Do you know if your father ever took a trip to Geneva or the Bahamas?"

"Course not," she said, locking a gaze on a confused Grant.

"How can you be so sure?" Grant asked, staring down at her,

hoping she realized his doubt had nothing to do with his lack of trust in her.

"Because—"

"He has aviophobia," Meeks stated before Autumn could answer.

Autumn tensed up. "How do you know about my father's fear of flying? He's very private about his condition. He thinks it's a sign of weakness."

"Meeks and his family own an international security and investigation company," Grant explained.

"Oh, I see." She fixed her eyes on Grant. "Now I know how you got my home address," she gave him a playful nudge with her elbow.

"No comment." Grant kissed her on the temple.

"My father only travels by train or car," she offered.

"Why is this so important?" Grant asked, pinning a gaze on her.

"The Alderman is dirty. Sorry, Autumn."

Grant tightened his hold, offering his support. "Go on."

"However, he's not responsible for what's been happening at the hotel." Meeks stated his voice strong. "He's being set-up. And so is Autumn."

"By who?" she asked.

"That's what Meeks and his team is working on finding out. They're the best too, trust me."

Autumn nodded and said, "I do." She returned to the chair she had abandoned and took a seat.

Grant took the phone off speaker and leaned against the desk. "Meeks, something else has come up."

He groaned, taking in a calming breath. "What now?"

"There's nothing for you to do, I just want to keep you in the loop." He smiled down at Autumn, reached for her hand and intertwined their fingers. "I was served with an injunction against the Castle today. It looks like the Maharaj family isn't taking the change in ownership lying down. They're using the Wilmette Historical Society trying to claim the Castle is being designated as an historical landmark. They've already started court proceedings to wrest control away from us. We can't let that happen. Ever."

CHAPTER 23

Grant entered Autumn's house carrying the woman he loved in his arms. They had barely crossed the threshold before they started tugging at each other's clothes. Grant knew they wouldn't make it to the bedroom, so he carried Autumn to the sofa. After placing her on the soft confines of the cushions, he stepped back and started stripping out of his clothes. Autumn sat wide-eyed, licking her lips.

Standing naked as the day he was born, Grant looked down at Autumn and said, "I'm going to undress you and make love to you until we're both too exhausted to move."

"Talk is cheap, mister," she taunted, gifting him with a sexy smile.

After removing Autumn's clothes faster than even he knew was possible, Grant sheathed himself in a condom. His heart pounded as he hovered over Autumn, throbbing to return to the only home he would ever want or know. Grant gripped her hips, thrust his engorged erection forward hard, setting a pace that plunged them both into a zone of pleasure. Their combined scents filled the room and before long, they both fell over the edge screaming out each other's name.

Grant carried a sated Autumn up the stairs and placed her on the bed where they made love again. After assuring she was sound asleep, Grant eased out of the bed. He stood gazing down at Autumn amazed at how much he'd come to love his woman. Grant walked naked downstairs where he gathered up their clothes. After slipping back into his briefs, he pulled his cell from his pants pockets and placed another call he'd been dreading.

"Grant, what's up?"

"Vikkas, we have a problem."

After bringing his brother king up to speed, the two agreed to meet with everyone the next day to discuss their next steps.

Grant was too close to having everything he never knew he wanted, and he wasn't going to let anyone, or anything get in his way.

* * *

Autumn sat up in bed with her back against the headboard, feeling like a woman who had been well loved. She still couldn't believe Grant wanted them to make a life together. But first they had to deal with her father and whoever else was coming after Grant. He told her about the mystery person's blackmail. She was honored that Grant meant what he said. There would be no secrets between them.

"Here we go." Grant walked into the room wearing only his briefs carrying two glasses and two opened bottles of wine; a Moscato for her and a Chardonnay for him.

"Two bottles, Grant?" She smiled up at him.

"Yes, you like the sweet stuff and the only thing sweet I love to drink is you." He leaned down and kissed her on the lips.

Autumn reached for and held both glasses as he filled hers, then his. She watched as he placed the bottles on the side table, removed his underwear, before joining her on the bed. She felt giddy inside knowing what was coming.

"I'd like to make a toast."

"Okay, what are we toasting to?" Autumn shimmed her shoulders.

Grant smiled. "To our future."

"I'll drink to that," she replied, tapping her glass against his and taking a sip.

He wrapped his arm around Autumn, pulling her into his side. "I've been thinking."

"Oooh, that must hurt," she teased.

"You've got jokes."

Autumn smiled up at Grant. "I think you need to confront my father with everything you have against him." She heard his deep sigh and saw the doubt about her suggestion in his eyes. "Hear me out. He'll know, or at least have an idea, of who's trying to set us up."

"I'm listening." He took a drink from the glass.

"I know my father's been double-dealing with folks in the community for years, a lot of politicians do, but he's also done a lot of good for people. Things weren't always done right way, but a lot of families and businesses in the in his ward prospered."

Grant's expression hardened and his jaw clenched. He stared down at Autumn and said, "What about all those who didn't make your father's preferred list? Those families and businesses that didn't even get a chance to be considered for projects like mine. Or those businesses who were on his *list*,"—he crooked his fingers like quotes—"but were limited to the amount of wealth they could gain because your father had to have his cut. A pretty damn big cut, too."

Autumn heard the disgust in his voice and knew he was right. She felt ashamed and embarrassed that she even tried to make an excuse for her father's behavior. "You're right, I'm sorry."

She could see Grant was upset with himself for letting his anger for her father get away from him.

"I'm sorry too." He took her glass and placed them both on the table. "I know this is hard for you. No matter what, he's still your father."

"I just…"

Grant kissed her gently on the lips. "What?"

"I know he may deserve it, but I just don't want to see him go to jail."

He looked down at the moisture misting in her eyes, strained face, and kissed her on the lips. "That's going to be up to him, sweetheart, but I'll try to help. For you."

"Oh, Grant. How can the best thing that ever happened in my life, come on the heels of the worst thing that could change my relationship with my father forever?" She pulled him down on the bed and their time for talking was over.

CHAPTER 24

Grant stood behind the bar in the Castle's game room and handed Meeks a beer. "Man, this place is incredible."

"Thanks," Grant replied, smiling. He was proud of everything the Kings had accomplished. Successful in their own right, each King had taken Khalil's directive and now dedicated their lives to righting the wrongs that were done in Khalil's absence, and taking up the cause of making the world around them a better place while supporting each other in the process.

"This king thing is a big deal," Meeks acknowledged.

"Yes, it is," he replied nodding.

"So, you and Autumn."

Grant couldn't help but smile. "What about us?"

"Haven't seen you become attached to any woman in all this time and I was beginning to wonder if—"

"I was gay?" Grant growled, feeling angered.

"No, I was beginning to wonder if you ever would. I wouldn't care if it wasn't a woman. Uncle Ben was an example that love doesn't always fit tradition and I'm pissed you'd think so little of me."

Seeing the sacrifices his uncle had made for him throughout the years and the challenges he suffered just being himself had made

Grant sensitive about the subject of sexuality.

"Sorry, man. I get a little defensive when it comes to that topic. The years of being bullied in school about my uncle, even though he wasn't in any relationships while I was growing up, have made me a bit touchy."

"So, it's real?"

"Very." He took a long pull from the special beer that Daron and Dro had somehow been able to procure. Trying to cool the fire that flowed through his body at the mention of Autumn's name. "As soon as we put this mess to bed, I'm going to ask her to marry me."

His eyebrows shot up, "Seriously?"

"Every king needs a queen, Meeks."

"Oh, I know that, but you're the one who was adamant about not getting married or having kids."

"That was before I met Autumn. I can't imagine my life without her, man."

"Damn." Meeks shook his head. "My wife was right, … again."

"Isn't she always," Grant teased.

"Yep, she's absolutely amazing," he conceded, his voice light.

"Who's amazing," Daron asked, entering the game room.

"Meeks' wife." Grant walked from around the bar, and the two men shook hands. He turned from his king brother to his friend. "Meeks, Daron Kincaid, but here we consider him King of Morgan Park."

The two men shook hands. "Congratulations on all your successes with the development of those much-needed security devices for women. My wife is very impressed."

"Thanks."

"We'd love to commission some of them for our clients."

"Word," Daron said with a nod.

Grant returned to the bar. "Want a beer?"

"Sure."

Grant pulled out another glass growler of Yuengling Hershey's Chocolate Porter and opened the top before handing it to Daron to pour a pilsner.

"Thanks. Damn. This is good," Daron said after taking a hearty sip.

"I need a case," Meeks stated.

"It's not for sale. And doesn't come in bottles. This one isn't delivered across the Indiana State line," Daron offered, raising his glass, admiring the beautiful coloring.

"Yet, we have it here, a new delivery every week and it's on tap." Grant grinned.

"What's having the ability to experience the best if we don't use all of our resources."

"For beer?"

"Damn skippy," Daron shot back, taking another taste and smacking his lips.

They all laughed.

The three men moved to sit at a tall bar style table. "So, where are we? I figured it was time the three of us got together and lay out everything and discuss next steps."

Meeks turned his attention to Grant. "We identified the woman in the video. Her name is Gina Paulson, and she's the daughter of—"

"Hunter Paulson," Daron interjected, earning questioning looks from both men.

"Yes," Meeks confirmed with a puzzled expression.

By Daron's resigned expression, Grant thought he may have a

little more information than they did.

"Hunter Paulson is Jimmy G's stepbrother. Hunter was the one who vouched for your uncle. If he hadn't, Jimmy G wouldn't have given him that loan," Meeks explained.

"Do we know why? I mean, why he helped my uncle." Grant asked, frowning.

"It was for personal reasons. Your uncle and Hunter had been in a pretty serious relationship for years before your parents died. Then suddenly, they weren't," Meeks stated.

Recognition dawned on Grant's face. "Uncle Ben ended their relationship to raise me," he concluded. He remembered how often his uncle would say it was the two of them against the world. For a long time, it had been, too.

"Yes, and it seems Hunter didn't take it too well," Meeks said, rubbing his hands down his face.

Grant shook his head. "What does that mean?"

"He took an overdose of pain medicine … killing himself."

"Oh, man," Grant whispered.

Daron lowered his head. "Damn."

"That's awful, but what does that have to do with who's blackmailing me and setting up the Alderman?" Grant asked no one in particular.

"This may help." Daron reached into the front pocket of his jacket and pulled out a letter-size envelope and handed it to Grant. "This is what your twenty-grand bought."

Meeks eyes flickered between the two men. "What is it?"

Daron finished off the last of his beer. "The leverage Gina Paulson, and whoever her partner is, had over Grant," he answered.

"Wait, *she's the blackmailer*?" Grant asked, frowning. "Why"

"I can only guess, but from what I could find out, she blames your uncle for her father's death." Meeks scratched his beard. "To confirm her motive and get the rest of your answers, you're going to have to speak to her yourself. We have enough for the authorities to bring her in on the hotel blackmail."

Grant eyed Daron for a few minutes. "Do I want to know how you got all your information?"

"No, but I can tell you that no one got hurt." Daron smirked. "Although Gina Paulson could use a better security system."

"Do you know what this is?" Grant asked, holding up the envelope.

"Not my business and my sources feel the same," he assured.

"We still don't know anything about who she's working with," Grant said, tapping the edge of the envelope.

"Actually, I think I know who her partner is and," Meeks checked his phone. "In about twenty minutes or so, we'll have the confirmation and proof we need."

"Great. On another note—"

"Sorry I'm late," Vikkas stated as he entered, scanning the game room. "I can't get over how cool this room turned out."

"Thanks," Grant replied pulling his brother king into a hug, before Daron did the same. Meeks offered Vikkas a friendly handshake.

"Does everyone know about what's happening with this injunction?" Vikkas glanced around the room taking in each man's expression and nods. "Good."

"You want a beer?" Grant asked.

"No, I'm good." He took a seat at the bar and turned the stool toward the others. "I talked to Dad and he actually laughed when I told him the family was trying to claim that the Castle was a historical landmark."

"He laughed?" Daron asked, frowning. "He's not taking this injunction serious?"

"No," Vikkas shook his head. "And neither should we according to dad. He'll make a few calls in the morning and put a plan in place that will have the whole thing squashed."

"Wait." Grant walked over and stood next to Vikkas. It was like he had to get closer to his brother king to make sure he was hearing him correctly. "What's going on Vikkas?"

"The family is right," he smirked. "A *piece* of the Castle is considered a historic landmark. It's just not as much as they think or what they detailed in the court documents."

"What do you mean?" Daron asked.

Vikkas pulled out his cell, flipped through a few pictures before he turned his phone for all to view. "This is what I mean."

Meeks scanned the images, then threw his head back and laughed. "Nice."

"What's so funny?" Daron asked, his gaze bouncing between Meeks and Vikkas. "It's a picture of a bridge."

"This bridge is the landmark and not the Castle or the land it sits on. Dad explained that bridge has been in the family for years." Vikkas smirked. "It has *special* meaning to him too."

Silence followed that admission.

"I'll give you three guesses as to why," he said laughing. "Actually, I won't. Let's just say Dad did a hell of a lot more on that bridge than cross it."

"TMI ... TMI," Daron said with a scowl.

"Well, Shaz always said that Khalil was a rolling stone. He just didn't realize the stones he had rolled on was a little close to home."

Daron pretended to zip his lips.

"So, we're good?" Grant asked rubbing his hands together.

"Dad is going to call their bluff."

"What good will that do?" Meeks asked.

"Trust me when I say, the Historical Society is not going to like what he has in mind."

"I think I have an idea because he asked me to send the exact requirements for a place to be designated a historical landmark," Grant said, laughing.

"He wouldn't," Daron said, also smiling.

"But they don't know that." Vikkas said with a grin of his own.

"By this time tomorrow the Historical Society will be on board," Vikkas assured. "I think I'll have that drink now."

Meeks' phone vibrated. He read the screen before forwarding the message and the attached files. "Grant, check your phone."

He pulled out his phone, read the message and the files. "Well, damn."

CHAPTER 25

True to his plan, Khalil had multiple construction crews surrounding the main parts of the Castle structures. Demolition equipment spread across the grounds, poised to dismantle a place that had been a fixture in Wilmette for decades. The screech of tires caused Khalil, the Kings, and the Knights to angle in the direction of the sound. Soon several other cars came through, following directly behind the first car as it pulled up into the empty parking lot.

A group of people left the cars, sprinting across the grass to reach the spot where Khalil and everyone held ground.

"What the hell are you doing," screeched Chris Allen, the president of the Historical Society, as his fellow board members fanned around him.

"You want The Castle to return to Wilmette's jurisdiction, stating that it is being classified as a historical landmark." Khalil presented his palms and plastered a smile on his handsomely chiseled face. "We are doing exactly as you asked."

Confusion marred the man's face. "But why are all these trucks and everyone else here?"

"Because they're going to take out every brick, every wall, every room and we will re-build it in another village where the status as belonging to these nine young men is absolute," Khalil explained, his expression closed up. "You want the landmark, you will have it. We want every ounce of blood, sweat and tears that went into making this place. You cannot have it both ways."

"You can't tear this down," a strawberry blonde said, gesturing to the men in hard hats who awaited their final instruction "It's illegal. This place is now a historical site. You don't have any jurisdiction here. We do."

"No, actually," Vikkas said, handing the president and the board members a set of the legal documents which were compiled with the help of Grant, Vikkas, Reno and Shaz. "Only the bridge falls under that designation. Everything else that was built around it, and even the land is solely the property of The Kings of the Castle and we can do whatever we like with our property."

"But—but—but it's worthless without everything else," Chris said, reading over the document he'd just received. Several of the members voiced their agreement.

"Not our problem," Grant said, placing a hand on Khalil's shoulder.

"And this isn't even the judge who is hearing the case," one of the members protested, tossing the paperwork to the ground.

"Yes, about that," Shaz said, stepping forward. "That particular judge has recused himself because he has the inability to be partial." His gaze shifted to the short, dark-haired man standing in the midst of the board members. "You can thank Najan Maharaj for that. That money was traceable, so ..." He shrugged and let the meaning carry. "Unfortunately for him, this new judge can't be bought."

"We didn't know anything about that," Chris said, his face darkened with anger. "And you would tear it down just to ... to spite us."

"It's not about you," Grant said coming to stand next to Shaz. "We're complying with the demand to relinquish the property to the Village of Wilmette."

"That means *all* of the property," Najan Maharaj protested, his tone as hard as the gleam in his eyes.

"No," Grant said, reaching over to flip the pages until he landed on the legal surveys that clearly indicated which parts of the land were built one-hundred years ago, and which parts were Khalil's construct.

"But it's not worth anything without all of the buildings on the property."

"Not our problem," the Kings chorused in unison.

"What they said," Khalil taunted with an amused smile.

"We obtained a court order that says the Castle property, grounds; all structures are to be ours."

Grant stepped forward. "Right and we have put in the amended motion that clarifies that you deliberately misled the court as to what is considered historical and what parts do not fit the criteria. I don't know who you paid off to submit those previous documents, but the judge is none too happy about the stunt you pulled."

"So here we are," Khalil chimed in. "We can move forward and tear it all down, leaving only that bridge, and have your organization foot the bill for all of it, per the judge's orders. Or you can leave us to our business and everything—all of it—stays intact."

"That would bankrupt us," Chris protested, gesturing to the work crews who were in various degrees of conversation.

"Yes, it just might," Grant said. "Either way, we are not walking away and leaving it to all of you."

Murmurs of discontent ensued as the board discussed their options."

"It stays," Chris said in a resigned tone as the other board members gasped in shock. "Don't tear it down."

Khalil signaled to the Kings, who spread out to inform the construction crews that there had been a change in plans.

"Great job son," Khalil said, pulling Grant into a hug.

"I'm glad this stunt of yours paid off."

"Me too," he replied, laughing.

Grant checked his watch. "I have to cut out. I have another important piece of business I have to handle."

Khalil gave a quick nod. "Go take care of your business."

* * *

Autumn stood in front of her desk looking over all the sports paraphernalia on her walls as she waited for her father to walk through the door. She wore a dark green sheath dress and a long-layered pearl necklace that had been her mothers'. It had been a gift from her father on her twenty-first birthday, and she touched her fingers to the cool surface, praying for strength.

"Good Morning, sweetheart." He kissed her on the cheek and the scent of his Gucci cologne came with him. "How's my beautiful daughter this morning?"

"Good Morning, father," she replied coolly, gesturing toward one of the chairs in front of her desk. "Please sit down."

"What was so important that you had to see me this morning?" He asked, taking the seat closest to Autumn.

"I need to talk to you about Richmond."

A wide smile spread across his face; his hands clasped as though he was holding back his excitement. "Let me guess, you've finally come to your senses and have accepted Richmond's marriage proposal. I couldn't be happier. He's a good man."

Her expression dulled. "No, Dad, he's not. Richmond and a woman named Gina Paulson have been blackmailing people. They went so far as to set things up to look like *we're the ones responsible*."

The color drained out of his face. He shifted in the chair angling closer to her. "Wh…what do you mean?"

"Just what I said. Richmond and Gina, or at least someone who worked for them, bugged the VIP rooms at your preferred hotel for your guests. When they heard or saw something that seemed worthy of blackmailing, they would, then put the money in an overseas account in *our* name. They extorted a lot of money from a number of people. And that doesn't include how you blackmailed Grant."

He flew out of his chair growling, "What are you talking about?"

Autumn took the seat next to her father. "Please, sit down. We don't have a lot of time."

The alderman stared down at her for several moments before complying. "What do you mean, *we* don't have a lot of time?"

"I mean, Grant will be joining us soon, and you'll need to be prepared to give him an answer that will change your life. What direction that takes will be up to you," she explained, keeping her disappointment at bay.

He reached for Autumn's hand. "What's going on?"

"Like I said, Richmond and this Paulson woman had someone working at Grant's hotel to put bugs and a camera in his room." She shook her head, grateful that Grand had reassured her that thanks to Meeks and Daron, no one had caught any of their private moments on video. "I guess, whatever you were asking for wasn't enough," she said with an accusing tone that made him bristle. "They must have been counting on getting something else incriminating that they could blackmail him on, too."

"I don't believe it."

"Why not?" she shot back. "You've done basically the same thing to all those folks on your preferred list of vendors. The people in our community trusted you for years."

"No, I have *helped* all those people on my list, and they love me," he insisted, his voice full of defiance. "You can ask any of them."

"I know you actually believe that, and while you were helping *some* people, you had your foot on the neck of others," she declared defiantly. "The people that never made your list. The ones that didn't make kickback payments. Disgusting. Mother would be ashamed of your actions. But we both know if she was still here, none of this would be happening. She must have been your moral compass."

The pain and sadness she felt manifested in tears she refused to release. She had to make her father see he was out of options if he didn't want to spend the rest of his life in prison.

The alderman opened his mouth, and then quickly closed it. He was clearly trying to think of an angle to justify what he'd done, but nothing would suffice.

"Richmond and Gina put their blackmail money in two banks out of the country in both of our names."

The realization of what that meant blossomed in his eyes. "What did you say?"

"Yes, dad, Richmond," she spat. "Your chosen one for son-in-law set us up to take the fall if anything went wrong."

She decided not to share Gina's motives and her connection to

Grant, letting him think money was their only reason for everything they'd done, knowing that was for the best.

"He wouldn't dare." His mouth set in a hard line; his face was expressionless.

Autumn heard the anger and doubt he tried to hide. "Why, Dad, because you taught him to be an *honorable* thief?" She gave a humorless laugh. "You might not have directly been part of *this* scheme, but your example showed him anything was possible."

"But he was like a son to me," he whispered, and his pained expression was almost laughable.

A knock at the door caused her to leave the desk.

"Yeah, well, your *son* is going to jail, and so are you if you don't take Grant's deal."

"What deal?" His eyes narrowed as he followed her movements. "And when did you team up with that bastard against your own father?"

Autumn opened the door and let Grant in. "Are you okay?" He cupped the side of her face with his right hand, and she nodded.

The alderman stood, shaking a fist at Grant. "Take your hands off her. What in the hell is going on here?"

"You need to listen to Grant, Dad," she warned. "He's going to help you if you let him."

He huffed, "Help me. It looks like he's already helped himself to you without my permission."

Autumn was in her father's face in two seconds and placed her hands on her hips. "*Your* permission. I'm a grown-ass woman, and I don't need your permission for anything, especially for who I choose to spend my life. You're my father, not my pimp. And you chose men who were corrupt, just like you."

He opened his mouth to respond but took in the angry glare and stance coming from Grant, and whatever he was about to say never made it past his lips.

Autumn moved away from him allowing Grant to step up and take over the conversation.

* * *

"Richmond has been arrested for extortion and money laundering. Gina Paulson has confessed to her role in the scheme and provided the authorities with evidence of Richmond's involvement," Grant explained giving the results from the information Daron received.

"I had no part in any of that," his voice had raised an octave along with both hands.

The surrender pose seemed appropriate.

Fear took hold in the alderman's eyes, and it was something Grant never expected. "We know, but you were more than complicit when you tried to blackmail me."

The alderman glanced over at Autumn. "That was a misunderstanding that Richmond brought to my attention. As the Alderman responsible for the contract, I had to address the issue. Thankfully, everything was rectified." He waved it off. "No harm, no foul."

Grant raised his left brow. "And your preferred list of vendors?"

The alderman shrugged. "It was merely a few solid recommendations."

"Recommendations." Grant felt the anger he'd been trying to control swirl inside of him like a hurricane. "Recommendations that kept several small family-owned businesses locked into a cycle that was just above poverty."

"Dad, please." Sadness crossed Autumn's expression.

The sound of her voice was like a calming blanket, warm and soft. Grant released an audible sigh. "Here's the deal, alderman. I have proof of your threat, but if you resign, I won't bring charges against you. You've done enough for your community. It's time to retire."

The alderman reached for the chair and slowly dropped into it. "So now you're blackmailing me?"

"No, I'm giving you a chance to stay out of prison," he warned. "A chance to meet your future grandchildren away from a glass barrier and out of prison gear."

The alderman glanced at his daughter. "You're siding against your very own father with this son-of-a—"

"No, she's trying to keep you out of prison," Grant stated, his anger coming through loud and clear. "If it weren't for Autumn, you'd be going to jail right now, alongside Richmond."

The alderman lowered his head and rubbed his hands together. He looked up and leered at Grant. "What's to stop Richmond from talking about *other* business that might be *questionable* to some people?"

"Nothing, but I'm sure you have enough of your own information against Richmond to keep him quiet." Grant watched as Autumn stood, her poker-face in place even though this had to be painful. "So, what's it going to be alderman?"

He stuck his nose in the air, slapped his hands against his knees, and stood. "I've done a lot for the city. Why not go out on top. My term ends in a year, that's plenty—"

Grant shook his head. "Your term ends today."

The alderman looked over at Autumn, who had her arms wrapped around her waist but remained silent. He turned his attention back to Grant. "I can't just quit like that. It would look … strange."

"You can, and you will," Grant insisted, tilting his head slightly. "You can feign illness, exhaustion, or whatever, but if you want to stay out of prison, you resign *today*."

CHAPTER 26

Autumn walked over to her father and placed a hand on his shoulder. "Please, daddy," she whispered.

"And," Grant began, tossing a set of documents to James Knight. "You'll need to sign these and have your lawyer execute the provisions."

Alderman Knight snatched open the envelope and pulled out the pages. "What provisions?"

"We had an accountant go over every backyard deal you managed to pull off. Ones that took advantage of the people in your ward." He gestured to the documents. "There's an amount that each one of these people are owed, and you're going to pay it, quietly. Or they're going to make some serious noise in the form of a class action lawsuit."

"I don't have to worry about that. No one knows the details anything I've done," the alderman protested.

"They will," Grant warned in a deadly tone. "I promise you. Mark's grandmother was caught in your web. He knows enough to make sure the spider is extinguished."

Minutes ticked by. His expression filtered through a range of emotions. "Okay, I'll do it for you." He hugged and kissed her on the forehead. Then walked over to Grant. "My daughter is very special."

"I couldn't agree more," Grant said, gazing into Autumn's eyes.

He gave Grant a quick nod and left the office.

Grant turned to Autumn, and she rushed into his outstretched arms. "Thank you."

He stared into her eyes. "I love you, and I'd do anything for you."

"I love you, too."

Grant gifted Autumn with a mega-watt smile. "Besides, I don't want to see my father-in-law in prison."

Her whole face lit up. "Father-in-law?"

"Yes, what do you think?" He ran the back of his hands down the side of her face. "Will you marry me?"

"Yes, I'll marry you." He picked Autumn up and spun her around. The sound of her laughter made everything in him come to life.

"Let's get out of here."

"Sounds like a great idea." Autumn wrapped her arms around his neck and pulled his face down for a passionate kiss sending her body up in flames. "I think it's time we close the book on the past."

"Agreed."

* * *

Grant stood in the living room of the two-story family home. He'd spent many wonderful years living in Texas. The expensive antique furnishings spoke to his Uncle's over the top personality. He smiled about all the times he'd been told to be careful when he'd sit on the Queen Anne chairs. Grant was gazing out of the sliding glass folding doors that brought the outside in, feeling nervous about the news he had come to deliver.

The last forty-eight hours had been a whirlwind of activity. Alderman Knight resigned, and Mark decided to throw his hat in the ring for the special election to fill the outgoing Alderman's position. With both Richmond and Gina behind bars, there was no longer a threat against Grant or his business.

The Castle was safe and still in the hands of the Kings who were determined to restore and maintain it at the level of excellence their mentor and father had intended.

Grant was on top of the world. Autumn was now wearing his ring on her finger. A ring that had once belonged to his mother, only he'd had the center stone replaced with a five-carat princess cut diamond whose brilliance was blinding. Autumn had been speechless. She'd thanked him with a kiss so passionate that it led to a night of unbelievable pleasure. Their love was on full display, and Grant was a happy man. Meeks teased him to the point where Grant had considered rescinding his offer of making him best man in his wedding. He did have eight others to choose from.

The only thing left for Grant to do was to return something that rightfully belonged to his uncle. Grant had finally gotten around to opening the envelope that Daron had given him, and his friend had been right. Retrieving the document was worth the twenty thousand dollars he paid. Hunter Paulson needed to be persuaded to help uncle Ben get the loan. Jimmy G was not the type of man to be played with, and he only dealt with family or people he knew personally.

Ben wanted to help his nephew get their construction company off the ground without having to tap into the trust fund he'd established with all the assets Grant had inherited from his parents—he'd been deemed a millionaire at the age of ten. Ben reluctantly used the interest earned from the trust fund to assist with Grant's upbringing, and for his education. He knew that would be the one thing his deceased brother would expect.

He was finding a way to get the funds needed to put them in the position to go after big-dollar contracts which became Ben's number one priority. They needed an infusion of cash, and he knew how to get the money, but it would require a sacrifice Ben was more than willing to make. He told Grant he would take out a second mortgage on the house, but he'd contacted his old lover for help.

Hunter Paulson agreed to get his stepbrother to loan Ben the money, but he wanted something in return. He wanted to rekindle their relationship, a secret, long-term, but long-distance affair. Hunter was a married man deep in the closet. He had one child, a daughter. As a token of his love and appreciation, Ben gave Hunter a percentage of his shares of the construction company. A company Hunter was proud to be a part of, and watch grow. The shares he received could only be sold back to the Khambrel family or revert to his beneficiary.

When Hunter died, those shares went to his only child. A child who resented her father and hated his lover. Her father had divorced her mother and settled for what she considered was a cheap affair with Ben. Gina blamed Ben for destroying the life she felt cheated out of, a life with parents who loved her and each other. She hated her father and wanted to destroy the one person she knew he loved more than anything. In her mind that included her, the home-wrecking man, the company, and the child he raised as if he was his own.

"Grant, Autumn is helping Sam with dinner. She said you wanted to speak with me," Uncle Ben said, sitting on the sofa.

"Yes, sir." He reached in his shirt pocket and pulled out the envelope. "This is yours."

His uncle accepted the envelope with a puzzled look on his face.

"What is it?" He asked as he peeled back the seal, his eyes widened. "How'd you get this, Grant?"

Grant spent the next thirty minutes explaining everything that had happened over the last few weeks.

Uncle Ben listened, and Grant tried to read his uncle's facial expressions. By his body language, he wasn't happy about being kept in the dark.

Minutes passed, and Grant allowed his uncle the space to process. "You should've told me."

"I didn't want to upset you and your recovery," Grant said, trying to defend his actions. "Jai said those treatments required complete calm."

Uncle Ben lightly ran his fingers across the envelope. "I gave Hunter a percentage of my shares of our company because I loved him."

Grant leaned against one of the wingback chairs facing his uncle. "Why did you choose to end things with Hunter? Did you think I wouldn't understand?"

"It wasn't your place to understand," he countered. "You were a ten-year-old who'd just lost both his parents. Your world had been shattered, and the last thing you needed was to feel like you were competing for my attention with anyone."

Grant held his gaze and fought back tears of love, appreciation, and admiration. His uncle had sacrificed his personal needs and wants for him, and he would always be grateful for giving him the time and attention he didn't even know he needed. Grant reached down, embraced his uncle and said, "I love you."

"I love you too, son." Sadness clouded his features. "I destroyed Hunter when I decided to end things before you came to live with me. We got back together when he agreed to help me get the loan. We even talked about trying to make a life together. Hunter left his family for me, but I'd just received the cancer diagnoses and wasn't emotionally ready for that type of commitment or felt it was fair to him. I had to focus all my energy on staying alive and being there for you. You know how hard things were back then."

Grant nodded. "I remember, hell, you were reluctant even to tell me what was going on. The move alone was hard on both of us, and I was getting ready to go to college. I was so scared of losing another parent figure. Thank God, I didn't."

"Thank God for that, but my decision caused a man to take his own life," he whispered.

Grant heard the remorse in his uncle's voice. "That was a decision Hunter made. It wasn't your fault." He paused a moment. "Can I ask you something?"

"Of course, you can," he said, sitting back further into the sofa. "But how about you sit down."

Grant took the seat across from his uncle. "Why did you decide to give Hunter shares of *our* company? I mean, I get that you loved him, but you could have just given him money if you thought he needed it."

"He didn't *need it*, but yes, I wanted him to have a financial safety net. Hunter took a huge hit financially when he got divorced. He lived well, but he'd never been a big saver or planner. I didn't ever want him to have to worry about money. I knew you'd make our company successful, so he'd be fine." He tossed the envelope on the table. "Besides, I set it up so that the only person those shares could be sold to is someone in our family."

"I'm guessing Gina didn't know that," Grant said, laughing.

Ben snapped his fingers. "She also didn't know who she was dealing with, either."

Autumn walked into the room. "Dinner's ready. Uncle Ben, Sam says not to forget your supplements."

"I swear that man." Ben stood shaking his head. "This is what marriage looks like, are you two ready for this?"

"Yes," they echoed and smiled at each other.

Ben left the room, laughing.

Grant walked up to Autumn and wrapped his arms around her waist. "I love you. My beautiful green-eyed queen."

She placed a kiss on his lips. "And I love you, my King of Lincoln Park."

King of Lincoln Park introduced you to Meeks and the Blake Sisters. Their stories are told in three Harlequin Romances, *Protecting the Heiress, Seducing the Heiress,* and *Tempting the Heiress.*

Protecting the Heiress

Stepping up as head of her family's international security firm gives Francine Blake, heiress and eldest Blake triplet, almost everything she's ever wanted. The one thing missing is the sexy, stubborn company partner who's been in her fantasies for too long. She refuses to give in to their attraction unless he can love her as his equal. But working together to safeguard a celebrity client is sweeping Francine closer to total surrender.

Security specialist Meeks Montgomery can think of any number of places he'd love to see gorgeous Francine every day. Behind her desk—fine. In his bed—even better. In the field on dangerous assignments? His heart can't stand it. Until a new case puts them both in the line of fire, proving how much he'd risk to be the one who protects her forever…

Seducing the Heiress Back Matter

Friends who flirt—that's corporate attorney Farrah Blake and high-tech security expert Robert Gold. Farrah, second of the wealthy Blake triplets, has no intention of acting on her attraction to the notorious bachelor. Until a business trip to Sin City turns into a wild and wanton weekend that leaves her with an unforgettable souvenir: a wedding ring!

Robert has made his share of romantic mistakes, but marrying the gorgeous, no-nonsense Farrah isn't one of them. Though he reluctantly agrees to her divorce request, he's hoping to change her mind. Trouble is, he'll have to deceive her in order to do it. And though all's fair in love and Vegas, gambling with the truth could cost Robert a love he's willing to stake his heart on …

Tempting the Heiress Back Matter

Back in med school, Felicia Blake couldn't help being impressed by Griffin Kaile's physique, as well as his intellect. The youngest of the accomplished Blake triplets, Felicia has put aside dating to focus on her career as a research scientist. She may have fantasized about Griffin—now a renowned cardiovascular surgeon. But that didn't include discovering that he's the biological father of the baby girl she's been asked to raise.

Even in scrubs, Felicia is the most stunning woman Griffin has ever known. Now that the daughter he never knew about has brought them together, he's eager to explore their romantic potential. But ambitious Felicia is reluctant to jump from passion to instant family. Which leaves Griffin only one choice—to somehow show her that this kind of breathtaking chemistry occurs only once in a lifetime...

More books by Martha Kennerson

Then Came You

India Slone has one thing on her mind, expanding her already flourishing advertising agency. That is until a wealthy University of Houston alum wills a valuable piece of land to the school and the adjacent community known as the Ward. The will states that only something that benefits both the school and the community can be built on the land. When India is asked to assist her alma mater in raising money and secure support for an education and job search resource center, she jumps at the opportunity.

Jonathon Victor, Chief of the City's Fire Department, has dedicated his life to service. As a third generation fireman, Jonathon understands the need to have the appropriate amount of firehouses embedded in the community. He also understands the city's difficulty in making that a reality. When Jonathon is approached to act as an advocate for a community service organization trying to raise money and support for a volunteer fire station and training center on the gifted land, he too accepts the offer.

When the two adversaries meet, they are struck by a surprising and uncontainable desire. Will unexpected and highly explosive passion lead to a compromise or all-out war?

His Biggest Fan

Dr. Tonya Banks spent her life focusing on her career and developing her craft. She followed all the rules, and it served her well. The successful ER physician heads one of the most prestigious hospital emergency rooms in the country. Finding love was never on her list of priorities. Dr. Charles "Chuck" Murphy is a world-renowned neurologist whose surgical talents are by far one of the best in the world. His skills in the operating room catapulted him to a level of success that only one other person always knew he would achieve, his best friend. Tonya and Chuck met in medical school and instantly became friends. They encouraged and supported each other, but their shared attraction remained secret and dormant.

Years later, a medical conference brought the two friends back together where they finally explored an unbridled passion. Their wild and sexy weekend ended, and they went back to their respective lives. What happened in Vegas stayed in Vegas; including surprising and still unreciprocated love. Nearly two years later, consequences of their scandalous weekend threaten the lives they each worked so hard to achieve. Will the good doctors finally put their past to bed and move on to their happily ever after?

Martha Kennerson

is a bestselling and award-winning author whose love of reading and writing is a significant part of who she is. She uses both to create the kinds of stories that touch the heart. Martha has penned and independently published two gripping novel Choices and Consequences based in part on her own experiences. Also, Martha has contributed to three additional books; Baring it All: The Ins and Outs of Publishing, Signed, Sealed, Delivered...I'm Yours and Spice, romance anthologies.

Most recently, Martha has developed gripping romantic stories that seduce, intrigue and step off the pages and into a reader's heart. The first in that endeavor, were two bestselling romantic series The Blake Sisters and The Kingsley's of Texas for the Harlequin Kimani line. Currently, Martha is in the process of developing a number of romantic novella's and a romantic suspense series, all scheduled to be released in 2019 and 2020.

Martha lives with her family in League City, Texas. She believes her current blessings are only matched by the struggle it took to achieve such happiness. She loves to interact with her readers. To find out more about Martha and to follow her writing journey, visit her website at www.marthakennerson.com or on Facebook, and Twitter pages @ KennersonBooks.

ABOUT THE KINGS OF THE CASTLE SERIES

Books 2-9 are standalones, no cliffhangers, and can be read in any order.

Book 1 – Kings of the Castle, the introduction to the series and story of King of Wilmette (Vikkas Germaine)

USA TODAY, New York Times, and National Bestselling Authors work together to provide you with a world you'll never want to leave. The Castle. Powerful men unexpectedly brought together by their pasts and current circumstances will become a force to be reckoned with. Their combined efforts to find the people responsible for the attempt on their mentor's life, is the beginning of dangerous challenges that will alter the path of their lives forever. Not to mention, they will also draw the ire and deadly intent of current Castle members who wield major influence across the globe.

Fate made them brothers, but protecting the Castle and the women they love, will make them Kings. www.thekingsofthecastle.com

King of Chatham - Book 2 - Reno
King of Evanston - Book 3 - Shaz
King of Devon - Book 4 - Jai
King of Morgan Park - Book 5 - Daron
King of South Shore - Book 6 - Kaleb
King of Lincoln Park - Book 7 - Grant
King of Hyde Park - Book 8 - Dro
King of Lawndale - Book 9 - Dwayne

Cover design by J. L. Woodson - www.woodsonstudio.com

ABOUT THE KINGS OF THE CASTLE SERIES

Books 2-9 are standalones, no cliffhangers, and can be read in any order.

Book 1 – Kings of the Castle, the introduction to the series and story of King of Wilmette (Vikkas Germaine)

USA TODAY, *New York Times*, and National Bestselling Authors work together to provide you with a world you'll never want to leave. The Castle. Powerful men unexpectedly brought together by their pasts and current circumstances will become a force to be reckoned with. Their combined efforts to find the people responsible for the attempt on their mentor's life, is the beginning of dangerous challenges that will alter the path of their lives forever. Not to mention, they will also draw the ire and deadly intent of current Castle members who wield major influence across the globe.

Fate made them brothers, but protecting the Castle and the women they love, will make them Kings.

www.thekingsofthecastle.com

King of Chatham - Book 2

While Mariano "Reno" DeLuca uses his skills and resources to create safe havens for battered women, a surge in criminal activity within the Chatham area threatens the women's anonymity and security. When Zuri, an exotic Tanzanian Princess, arrives seeking refuge from an arranged marriage and its deadly consequences, Reno is now forced to relocate the women in the shelter, fend off unforeseen enemies of The Castle, and endeavor not to lose his heart to the mysterious woman.

King of Evanston - Book 3

Raised as an immigrant, he knows the heartache of family separation firsthand. His personal goals and business ethics collide when a vulnerable woman stands to lose her baby in an underhanded and profitable scheme crafted by powerful, ruthless businessmen and politicians who have nefarious ties to The Castle. Shaz and the Kings of the Castle collaborate to uproot the dark forces intent on changing the balance of power within The Castle and destroying their mentor. National Bestselling Author, J.L. Campbell presents book 3 in the Kings of the Castle Series, featuring Shaz Bostwick.

King of Devon - Book 4

When a coma patient becomes pregnant, Jaidev Maharaj's medical facility comes under a government microscope and media scrutiny. In the midst of the investigation, he receives a mysterious call from someone in his past that demands that more of him than he's ever been willing to give and is made aware of a dark family secret that will destroy the people he loves most.

King of Morgan Park - Book 5

Two things threaten to destroy several areas of Daron Kincaid's life— the tracking device he developed to locate victims of sex trafficking and an inherited membership in a mysterious outfit called The Castle. The new developments set the stage to dismantle the relationship with a woman who's been trained to make men weak or put them on the other side of the grave. The secrets Daron keeps from Cameron and his inner circle only complicates an already tumultuous situation caused by an FBI sting that brought down his former enemies. Can Daron take on his enemies, manage his secrets and loyalty to the Castle without permanently losing the woman he loves?

King of South Shore - Book 6

Award-winning real estate developer, Kaleb Valentine, is known for turning failing communities into thriving havens in the Metro Detroit area. His plans to rebuild his hometown neighborhood are derailed with one phone call that puts Kaleb deep in the middle of an intense criminal investigation led by a detective who has a personal vendetta. Now he will have to deal with the ghosts of his past before they kill him.

King of Lincoln Park - Book 7

Grant Khambrel is a sexy, successful architect with big plans to expand his Texas Company. Unfortunately, a dark secret from his past could destroy it all unless he's willing to betray the man responsible for that success, and the woman who becomes the key to his salvation.

King of Hyde Park - Book 8

Alejandro "Dro" Reyes has been a "fixer" for as long as he could remember, which makes owning a crisis management company focused on repairing professional reputations the perfect fit. The same could be said of Lola Samuels, who is only vaguely aware of his "true" talents and seems to be oblivious to the growing attraction between them. His company, Vantage Point, is in high demand and business in the Windy City is booming. Until a mysterious call following an attempt on his mentor's life forces him to drop everything and accept a fated position with The Castle. But there's a hidden agenda and unexpected enemy that Alejandro doesn't see coming who threatens his life, his woman, and his throne.

King of Lawndale - Book 9

Dwayne Harper's passion is giving disadvantaged boys the tools to transform themselves into successful men. Unfortunately, the minute he steps up to take his place among the men he considers brothers, two things stand in his way: a political office that does not want the competition Dwayne's new education system will bring, and a well-connected former member of The Castle who will use everything in his power—even those who Dwayne mentors—to shut him down.

AUTHOR BIOS

Naleighna Kai is the *USA TODAY* Bestselling Author of Every Woman Needs a Wife, Open Door Marriage, Loving Me for Me, Slaves of Heaven and several other controversial novels. She is founder of NK Tribe Called Success, The Cavalcade of Authors, and is a publishing and marketing consultant. www.naleighnakai.com

S. L. Jennings is a military wife, mom of three, coffee addict, Willy Wonka enthusiast, and real-life unicorn. She's also the New York Times and USA Today Bestselling author of Taint, Fear of Falling and the Se7en Sinners Series, along with a few other titles that she's too lazy to type. She's been with her high school sweetheart for almost twenty years, and he still can't get her Subway sandwich order right. But he's cute and brings her vodka, so she keeps him around. They currently reside in Spokane, WA with their three stinky boys and their equally stinky cat. www.sljenningsauthor.com

Martha Kennerson is the bestselling and award-winning author who's love of reading and writing is a significant part of who she is. She uses both to create the kinds of stories that touch the heart. Martha lives with her family in League City, Texas. She believes her current blessings are only matched by the struggle it took to achieve such happiness. To find out more about Martha and her journey, visit her website at www.marthakennerson.com and you can follow her on Facebook and Twitter.

J. L. Campbell is an award-winning Jamaican author who has written over thirty books in several romance subgenres. Campbell, who features Jamaican culture in her stories, is a certified editor, and also writes non-fiction. Visit her on the web at www.joylcampbell.com.

National bestselling author, **Lisa Watson**, is a native of Washington D.C., and writes in the Multicultural & Interracial, Contemporary, Romantic Suspense, and Sweet Romance genres. Her memorable novels for the Harlequin's Kimani line, The Match Broker series was listed as one of 2014's Top 25 Books of the Summer, and Top 50 Best Reads. Lisa lives in Raleigh, North Carolina with her husband of twenty-two years and two teenagers, and is avidly working on book one, Alexa King: The Guardian, in her second new Romantic Suspense series, The Lady Doyen and Book 2 in the Love and Danger Series. www.lisawatson.com

Karen D. Bradley is a national bestselling author and screenplay writer. English and Grammar were never her strongest subjects, but as life would have it, her weakest link would become her saving grace. Writing fiction became one of her favorite forms of therapy. She has penned several contemporary fiction, suspense, and romantic suspense novels. Visit Karen on the web at www.karendbradley.com

Janice M. Allen is a National Bestselling Author who has always been an avid reader of fiction. She even edited the work of other authors for several years. But she gets an incomparable thrill from creating stories that entertain readers and cause them to reflect on real life issues. No Right Way To Do A Wrong Thing is her first novel, followed by her short story Cayenne. www.janicemallen.com

London St. Charles has always had a passion for the pen, paper, and books. She is a Chicago native who uses the Windy City as a backdrop to the romance, suspense, and contemporary fiction stories she writes. London published her debut novel, The Husband We Share in 2017 and is one of nine authors in the anthology, Sugar. She also composes an online newsletter, London Writes, that keeps readers abreast of what's going on in her world. www.londonstcharles.com

MarZe Scott is a lifelong resident of Ypsilanti, Michigan and Graduate of University of Michigan. A lover of all things creative, MarZé enjoys reading, free-hand illustrating, jewelry making and makeup artistry.

Known for her vivid and captivating storytelling, MarZé has been writing short stories and poems since elementary school and developed a taste in high school for writing about provocative topics like the consequences of casual sex. You can find Gemini Rising, MarZé's debut novel, and short story Next Lifetime wherever books are sold. www.marzescott.com

SERIES MENTORS:

LaVerne Thompson is a *USA Today* Bestselling, award winning, multi-published author, an avid reader and a writer of contemporary, fantasy, and sci/fi sensual romances. She loves creating worlds within and without our world. She also writes romantic suspense and new adult romance under the pen name Ursula Sinclair also a USA Today Bestselling Author. www.lavernethompson.com

Kassanna is a strong believer in love at first sight and happily ever afters. Writing has always been her passion but fate sometimes has other roads that must first be taken .Navigating the road less traveled was not only unexpected but in the end extremely rewarding. Her books are mainly contemporary romance but she has delved into the paranormal, fantasy, and plans on expanding into other areas as the ideas come to her. Right now she is enjoying life and seeing her works come into fruition make it that much more pleasurable especially when her books make others smile. Kassanna wouldn't have it any other way. www. flavorfullove.com